MAGIC LANDS:

JOURNEY

BEYOND THE

BEYOND

WRITTEN BY

ROBERT STANEK

This is a work of fiction. All the characters, names, places and events portrayed in this book are either products of the author's imagination or are used fictitiously. Any resemblance to any actual locale, person or event is entirely coincidental.

Reagent Press
Published by Virtual Press, Inc.

Cover design & illustration by Robert Stanek
ISBN 1-57545-064-X

Also by Robert Stanek

Magic Lands
Journey Beyond the Beyond
Into the Stone Land

Keeper Martin's Tales
The Kingdoms & the Elves of the Reaches #1, #2, #3 and #4
In the Service of Dragons #1, #2, #3 and #4

Ruin Mist Tales
The Elf Queen & the King #1, #2, #3 and #4

Ruin Mist Heroes, Legends & Beyond
Magic Lands & Other Stories

MAGIC LANDS: JOURNEY BEYOND THE BEYOND

BY

ROBERT STANEK

Table of Contents

MAGIC LANDS: JOURNEY BEYOND THE BEYOND

BY ROBERT STANEK

A Palisade:

A fence set firmly into the ground.
Like any fence, it keeps things out.
But it can also keep things in.

Chapter One:
The Quest Begins

Ray jumped from rooftop to rooftop, taking care not to disturb the residences therein. He journeyed to the land beyond the hill this day, a place he had never been. In some ways he was frightened by the prospect of his journey, yet in other ways he was overjoyed. For unlike all the other days he had known before, this day was like no other. This day, he left the village a boy but would return a man. *If he could prove himself. If he survived the journey. If he could remember. If he could forget. If, if, if.*

So many doubts, he thought to himself, *so much to do*. He must prove himself a man. He must remember everything the village smoot had told him. He must forget the dream of the wizard.

A baritone moan not far off startled him and he scrambled to regain his footing. He had been thinking too much, and not watchful of placement of foot or of his surroundings. *You are beyond the safety of the village,* he reminded himself, *a mistake, a misstep, and you are done for. Your journey will end before it has even begun.*

Again mindful of his step, he twisted the six-foot stretch of arbor in his hands, using it to poke and prod ahead. The answering calls of watchful bulls did not startle him now. He had been waiting for the returning calls, and to hear that of the one closest to him. He knew they hunted him. He did not mind; at times he hunted them. He knew of a place lost and deep where the bulls and the slithers gathered. This was the place he went to now, though it was far from the place he would eventually seek.

Two hours before dawn the village smoot had told him to go, and he had, saying his good-byes to those he held dear and heading out into the darkened land alone, his heart heavy with the thought that he would never see his home, friends or family again. He had never wanted to leave. He had told no one of the dreams. The dreams in which he walked amongst the Out. He did not want to walk amongst the out; he wanted to stay with those of the In, those of his kind, to the ends of his days. Most of all, he didn't want to meet the wizard, as it seemed fated he must do.

To those who asked, he had not readily admitted that he had dreamt of the Out—the place where the land did not quiver and shake with every footfall, the mourning step on ground that was not his own. He had said simply, "My path is long," and none had inquired further. Then, he had perceived himself smug for speaking this way. Now was frightened by the sound of his own words in his ears. His path was long, too long the village smoot had said. Too long to be safe. Too long to ensure his return to the village. Too long for the village smoot to see the path's end.

An enormous bull rushed from the depths of the nearest pool. He saw its movement beneath the water just before it broke the surface and avoided yearning eyes and grasping lunge by switching down a different avenue. A moment later, his eyes were bright and full of fire as he slipped to meet the wet with a splash. As he danced within the folds of the wet, his thoughts spun—the bull was large and swift, and only one house over. This was the mistake the village smoot had warned him of. This was the mistake that would cost him his life.

He scrambled to reach safety, scrambling for his very life. He wondered if the bull would come for him before he had a chance to pull himself out of the wet and return to the dry. He also wondered if the bull did, would his journey end before it had even begun?

He clasped his staff long. It was his truest companion and it had saved his life many, many times. Six feet was an impressive length, and it had been his choosing, for he had impressive yearnings. There were others like Tall who had chosen larger, but he still held that his choice was the best. At the time of selection, he had been a full foot and a half smaller, so it had been a hefty yearn to want such a sizeable staff. And this great staff—the product of his greatest yearning— wouldn't let him down. He wouldn't let it let him down.

He swung up, shuffling his feet as he had been taught and had learned was best. He could feel the bull at his feet just then. He poured strength into his arms, shifted the staff, hastened his feet to move as never before, and begged the lord of the heavens to spare him. A sudden explosion of pressure in his legs told him the bull's great jaws had found him. He planted the staff in the shallows of the muck and tried to hold on.

His heart beat so fast it was the only sound he could hear even as he screamed as he had never screamed before, even as he imagined what the loss of his legs would mean, even as he imagined the bull dragging him to the depths of the pool and his death.

Suddenly the wet was all around him. Just before he was pulled under, he found himself looking up at the heavens and in that brief moment he saw the last thing he imagined he would ever see: the sun breaking the horizon in the east, pink and orange spread across the heavens as if Tall had painted it there just for him, just so it would be the last thing he ever saw.

But it wasn't to be his final memory. No. The vision of the wizard came to him again. He saw the wizard towering over him as he clung to the barren rock at the top of what the smoot had told him was a mountain. *A mountain*, just the thought of it had excited him. He had never seen a mountain, no one in his village had ever seen a mountain, yet he had described the mountain and the wizard in enough detail for Tall to draw both. It was the drawings that brought the elders to him, the drawings that convinced the village smoot it was time for him to begin his journey.

As the vision faded, Ray realized he was no longer moving backward through the water. The bull had come to a rest on the bottom of the pool. Isaac's father had told him the story of a boy who had escaped from a bull. In the story, as the bull came to rest on the bottom, it adjusted its grip and the boy escaped. Sure enough as Ray and the bull started to sink slowly into the muck at the bottom of the pool, the bull relaxed its grip and then opened its jaws. Ray swam free, not realizing that to the bull this was little more than a game it played before stuffing its gutted prey under a log or rock for safe keeping.

One thing the bull didn't count on was that Ray's pack was sealed and airtight. The bit of air in the pack gave Ray extra buoyancy as he swam for his life. Soon he was breaking the surface of the pool.

He swam hand over hand, trying frantically to reach the dry shore which was only a few feet away. He found his staff wedged in the muck of the shallows like an out of place tree. He gripped it just as he sensed the bull was upon him again. This time he didn't hesitate. This time he swung his staff with all the strength he had left and hit the bull smack on the top of its head, right between its eyes. The bull looked up at him as if surprised, then rolled on its side and disappeared beneath the dark waters of the pool.

He shook a fist at the bull as it came to the surface again and stared it in the eye as he backed away warily, calling out, "I am not afraid of you, Old Bull. I've got lots to do this day and I'll not have you stop me. I'm leaving now, you best not follow, or I'll give you more of the same."

He was exhausted, but he couldn't rest. He wouldn't let himself rest.

He took quick inventory of his belongings and himself. His pack was intact. His staff, whole. He was wet. His leather skin boots were shredded. He slipped out of them and discarded them without a second thought. It seemed he could feel a few suckers on his skin. *No matter*, he told himself. He would deal with the suckers later. They wouldn't drink much of his blood and he could pull them off later—later when the bull was well behind him.

He trudged on. After a time, he came upon a gritty bush and claimed a large portion of its leaves for his own, careful to tender some but not all, thus allowing the cycle of growth to continue. He had seen the outsiders come to gather these and theft the wet. Their hair was fair and straight, straight and long like their faces and their lanky bodies. He thought the outsiders odd. To be quick and nimble, one needed to be thin; to hunt, one needed to be dark of eye and of skin; and as for hair, he saw no use for curl-less spans, his own closely manicured dark locks sufficed.

He used the grit to wash his hands, grinding it between his palms until it foamed, cautiously rinsing his hands in the wet. He allowed the dark images to fall from his eye as he did so. He feared the outsiders, almost as much as he feared and revered the shifting of the earth beneath his feet.

Coming to a house he knew, he slowed his gait to a walk. This was a spot he had marked in his mind. He had wanted to come here.

He navigated the house's bounds, questing for a small,

scented object, which he had been reminded to collect. He dug amongst thick folds now. The plant was not easily had, for it guarded its secrets well, as did those who used it. No one would visibly mark its whereabouts, though most knew where it grew in dotted paths nestled near and far.

He smiled as he found it, touching it gingerly and respectfully. The scent was sweet, the touch stinging, if not handled properly.

The bull cried out again, and Ray knew it was time to move on. "I'm not afraid of you, Old Bull," he said again to calm himself, not realizing until just then how alone he felt, and was. He switched residences, smiling as he encountered a sudden soft spot midway along his path.

"You never know," he whispered to the slight breeze, repeating words the old smoot had told to him just before he had gone off. "You never can be sure when you step that the ground will be there. Pay your respects I say. Watch out for Old Bull and his queen and you'll be okay."

Seeing the crafty eyes of a waiting slither, Ray skipped one house over. He fancied the way it lashed out its tongue, and the way it could wrap and twine. He prodded with his stick, detouring around a tender spot. He pictured Tall, a friend whom he missed. Tall was back at the village, waiting for his time to go out and make his mark—a time that was yet days off.

Recalling the next item on his list, Ray froze, scratching his chin. He attempted to remember which direction he should turn to find it. He veered right.

Passing a small, wiry bush, he broke off a bit of its slender branches, pocketing a small stash, slipping a small tender section between lip and jaw. The taste was sweet and bitter; this was the bittersweet. Ray puckered his lip; he liked the bittersweet. He took a couple of steps forward, passing to the very edge of the residence before turning back. He went back to the bush, claiming more of its tender leaves and branches for his own, until, finally satisfied, he turned away. Still, this wasn't the thing he sought and now he turned his attention back to the search for the next item on his list.

He skipped two houses down and one over, maneuvering ever with care on happy feet. He swung his staff from left to right for balance, using it to help him along his way. He tightened the straps on his pack, checking its seals by feel, right thumb and forefinger against the pack's edge.

The sun was fully over the horizon now, and he paused long enough to admire it while his eyes adjusted to the full light of the new day. Thinking of the slither and the bull, Ray wondered which he would choose when the time came. He knew the tiny creature he would choose would be his only companion on the long road to manhood and perhaps the greatest friend he would ever have, but he still didn't know in his heart of hearts which was for him.

Movement behind him scattered his thoughts. A fresh bull was on his trail. As he hurried to get out of the way, he heard a challenging call not far off. "This one is mine," warned Old Bull.

Ray didn't turn back. He knew it was best to let them play. Regardless which would gain the hunting rights, Ray knew he was both quicker and smarter, and nothing would stand in his way.

As the sun climbed into the sky, Ray's neighborhood sprang to life. He put urgency into his step now. He searched for a long rooted plant with a plump, leafy-green plume. He almost thought he might never find it. He needed it so. But no sooner had the thought occurred than he realized he was staring straight at a small group of leafy-green plumes. He snatched up his share and moved on.

Off in the distance, Ray saw a small, black speck. He knew this was the arbor tree of Second Village. He would steer wide of it or so he thought for a moment.

He stopped, resisting the urge to trudge on. He thought of comforts and good things—the good things he could find in Second Village. He thought of dry clothes and new boots. He thought of a warm meal and a warm drink. He needed it all; wanted it all.

"No, no. I mustn't go that way," he whispered to himself.

He couldn't continue though. Seeing the village reminded him of comforts, of home, of everything he was leaving behind. It also reminded him of what he had almost lost—his life. He started to kneel, then moved to sit, but collapsed to the ground in a ball instead.

Tears flowed down his cheeks. He cried in great sobs. He cried for what he was about to lose, for what he had almost lost, and for reasons he couldn't explain. *Ray, the quest has only begun,* he told himself. The voice he heard in his ears was not his own though, it was that of the great elder of his village, the smoot.

Taking a deep breath, Ray forced himself to stand. He turned his back to Second Village and walked away. It was then as he headed away from Second Village that he realized he would miss the hunt as well. The full heat of the day was coming. Old Bull would soon break off the hunt, and then Ray would have nothing to keep his tired feet moving.

Ray pushed down with his staff before he jumped to provide the extra power needed to reach the next house over. Whispered words of the old smoot came to his mind as he landed safely on the other side of the wet. "Put the sun to your back," the smoot had said, "Keep it there and go until you think you can't go any more, and then go just a little bit more..." Ray smiled. He liked the smoot.

The day continued as days do and soon Ray was at the end

of his list. As he didn't need to collect anything more, Ray found a safe, hard spot and waited out the hot of the day.

His feet were tired and his back ached, so he slipped the shoes from about his feet, rinsing them in the wet before he put them back on. He rummaged through his pack, double-checking the contents against his list. He searched right down to the gritty weed in the bottom of the pack. Satisfied, he settled in and started to make a bit of stew. He snapped a piece of dark root in two, crumbled the leaves from a small branch of bittersweet, mixed these into a container filled with a bit of the wet. Food for a trek, food to keep one on their feet, he thought to himself as he ate.

Afterward, he bunched up his pack and swung it onto his shoulders. He looked back at the sun for a moment and to a dark speck he imagined somewhere low beneath it that was the great arbor tree of Second Village. He decided then that he would miss Ephramme, Isaac and even Keene. But most of all he would miss Tall, whom he envied.

He had just stepped across the wet to the next patch, when he spotted a group of light root. He thanked his good fortune. He liked the light root, and he would have started to whistle if he had not heard the gentle splash beside him. His eyes lit up and a smile touched his lips.

"Still there, Old Bull?" he called out, leaping out of the way, thrusting his staff behind him as he went. A deep warbling groan called back to him. Ray laughed happily now.

"Come on, Old Bull," he yelled over his shoulder, "Catch me if you can!"

He traveled along imagined avenues through blocks and neighborhoods he did not know. He shifted his pack now and again until the weight settled comfortably on his back. He knew that soon he would find himself on mourning ground. A place where the ground did not tremble and quake beneath his feet. The place that was the land beyond the hill. The place where the wizard of his dreams dwelled. This excited him. This frightened him. And being both excited about a thing and frightened by it confused him greatly. He decided right then that if there was one thing becoming a man meant, he hoped it meant that he would no longer be confused by the things he did not understand and that he would be less confused by the things he thought he understood.

Chapter Two:
The Deep

Keeping the sun at his back had turned him in a relatively wide arch, and by the time it was hugging the horizon low behind him, Ray was exhausted. No one had told him it would be easy, but then again no one had told him it might take more than one day to reach the place lost and deep, and in a way, he was disappointed. He had been looking forward to this day for so long, and now it seemed that he would have to wait another day.

The thought of a night alone in the deep did not frighten him so much as worry him. He would have to find a safe place, and soon.

Thinking deeply and hurrying, he misplaced his step. The wet was quick to gather him in. He crossed out with his staff, bracing his fall so he did not sink too far, and then he carefully lifted his heavy body. He didn't see the bull until he placed a reassuring hand on the dry, and in fact, he had almost wandered straight into the other's abode.

He stared the bull in the eye, quickly thrashing the space between them. This one was smaller than the one who was his companion, though not his companion of choice. He didn't have time to ponder the other's whereabouts; he would have to deal with this one first. This bull was younger and swifter than Old Bull, who was craftier and wiser.

Snapping jaws and lurching tail were Ray's primary concerns. He used the end of his staff to rap the bull, a stout blow on his snout in the tender spot between the eyes.

The bull was wary but not excessively so. "I'm sorry to have invaded your home, I will not do so again, if you let me go," he called out. He was stuck. He couldn't jump backwards, a return trek into the wet now would be fatal and he couldn't get around the bull without a struggle.

He thudded the ground as hard as he could, prancing the stick from left to right. "Stay there," he cautioned, "One moment and I'll be gone, if you oblige."

White teeth glistened against the red-fire light of the setting sun. Tiny balls of perspiration licked Ray's brow, but the smile had not faded away—he was somehow excited by this encounter and not frightened as he had been before.

Renewed vigor surged through him. "If you eat me, you'll get a belly ache, this I promise you!" he teased. *One step right,* he told himself, moving gradually in that direction. Soft mush beneath his feet told him to retreat to the left.

His hands were trembling now as he rapped the bull again, coaxing it to scamper right. *One step left,* he told himself.

He saw the bull's eyes flash just as the beast's tail lashed at him. He braced himself, using the stick as he had been taught. His eyes became wide, ripe circles and his mouth dropped open as he fell. He was left staring into the eyes of the young bull and swallowed a hefty lump in his throat.

Somehow, he knew this was the end. Testing your luck twice in one day was much too much. The young bull would lash out with its tail, set its jaws upon him, and that would be that. But the young bull didn't move. It just looked at him. In the wet behind him, Ray heard a nearby splash and the deep rumbling challenge of Old Bull.

The challenge set Ray's feet to work. He jumped away, running for all he was worth, and did not stop running until he was half a dozen houses away. He glanced back then, searching for a dark shape in the wet, mumbling hurried thanks before he continued. He was not one to easily forget debts owed, and guessed that perhaps Old Bull would one day get his reward, but not if he was quicker.

A closely woven section of brambles spread out in front of him, again forcing him to detour. The tangled area was several blocks long and he would have to make a full circle around it. The sun was settling from the sky, brambles before him and bulls behind him, Ray stopped and took a deep breath. He cleared his thoughts, focusing on his goal: a place to safely spend the dark hours of night.

In navigating around the thick undergrowth, he came upon a beleaguered, time-bent tree, whose trunk sagged heavily. The ground here was hard and he saw no sign the residence was occupied. Moving his back up against the trunk so that his eyes faced the wet, he settled in for a while.

"My path is long," he whispered to himself, suddenly considering all that was ahead of him. Tomorrow, he was sure, would be a day of choosing.

He unclasped his pack and inspected its goods once more, white root, dark root, bittersweet, gritty bush, and all, claiming the second piece of dark root, a small piece of white root, a stalk of bittersweet, and one leaf of the gritty. "Mealtime," he told himself.

Before he washed his hands, arms and face with a bit of the wet and the gritty, he placed his prized meal on top of his pouch, and then strolled over to the edge of his newfound house.

He rinsed off, cautiously eyeing the wet for signs of slither and bull, and then wandered back to his little spot, considering many things. The slither was fast and sleek; it could wrap and entwine. The bull was quick of jaw and of tail, ferocious in most respects, a large mound of teeth and tail. Choosing the correct companion spoke as much about the questor as did the quest or the staff, and he knew this well. He had hefty yearns. He knew what he wanted in the end and to where he roamed, but still had not made the one choice that mattered most—the choice of companion.

Placing his back against the aged trunk, he slid to the hard ground. As he shifted his back against the tree, he felt and heard the squish as several plump somethings as thick wet splotches exploded across his back. Remembering his fall into the pool, he turned away from the tree as if it had bitten him, then began pulling off his clothes. The suckers were up and down his legs, under his arms, plump and ripe with his blood. His stomach soured and he gagged—something about suckers when they were fed full with blood always made his stomach queasy. Fortunately, he hadn't eaten much all day and there wasn't much to spit up.

After he wiped the spittle from his cheek and lips, he set about removing the suckers. Peeling them off wasn't as easy as it seemed. Suckers latched on to skin like they had a thousand tiny teeth. The remedy in his backpack was quite simple—the stinging. Wipe the stinging over them; they curled and writhed as if in pain. All you had to do then was to pluck them off and discard them.

When he used the stinging on all the suckers he could reach, he used the tree to squish those that remained in places he couldn't reach. Sudden pops, not unlike the popping of corn, and a bit of pain told him of his success. Afterward, he dress quickly and tried to put the grisly sounds of popping suckers out of his mind by eating.

He supped on a bit of light and a bit of dark, following it with the bittersweet—all of it meant to calm his nerves and settle his stomach. Crunching, slowly and quietly, he whittled away the time until the sun disappeared from view. He massaged tense muscles now, inspecting his feet for sores or worse. He found only one black sucker remained, perched between the big toe of his right foot and his next larger toe. He coaxed it off with the stinging, snuffed its life with the butt end of his stick.

Finding another sucker, set him back to searching. He ran his fingers under his arms and through his hair. He removed shirt and wrap, checked his back and genitals again just to be sure. Finding nothing, satisfied, he slipped back on his shirt and wrap, settling again against the old tree.

The air turned cool as the humidity lifted. He crouched low, bunching arms and legs close together. His eyes gradually acclimated to the changing light and he was less afraid. For a time, he remained motionless, eyes keen and ears alert. Hearing no movement, no slither, he relaxed, confident his abode was true.

The day sounds faded away, and the night sounds took their place. No more trumpeting of birds, or scampering of lesser creatures, although he did hear an occasional plop into the wet--not large plops mind you, rather, small ones. For a long while, he was too restless to sleep, contemplating a host of thoughts, each one grander than the last. His thoughts flared as he recalled something he had overlooked. He groped for the top of his pack, unsealing it and cautiously probing inside, immediately recalling why it was fruitful to have segregated the contents.

Cautiously he lifted four leaves of the stinging, placing them in a semi-circle around him at arm's length. A pungent, sweet aroma wafted to his nose, and now, he could sleep. He slept in the fashion of the In when in a strange place: eyes open, face held up and alert, though within his mind he drifted immediately into a pleasant sleep. He would later recall the things that had passed before his eyes in the night, as one would a dream.

Many hours later, a dull gray probing into his eyes told him morning had arrived. The sun was still far from the sky, but dawn had indeed settled in as he stirred. He gathered up the four leaves of the stinging and placed them tenderly back into his pack. As breakfast was the most important meal of the day for him, and in need of a plentiful supply of energy, Ray ate heavy, allowing a full root of dark and a half of the light. He drowned his thirst with as much of the wet as he could drink.

Excitement mixed with elation drove him to a frenzied start. Staff in hand, pack in place, he marched off. An unsettling, resonant splash just one residence over told him he was not alone this morning. He imagined it was still Old Bull in search of his prey, which helped maintain the urgency in his pace for many hours. The rooftops were hanging thick with dew, not unusual for the early morning hours, yet nevertheless, irritating to his skin as he went on his way.

He came to a widening, an area where the dry spread out sparsely, and it required much time and patience to by-pass. He had to make three trips through the wet, cringing with each, and counting his blessings after each. It was in places such as this where he gained renewed faith for the long stick he toted, for without it, he would have disappeared into innumerable deeps and never surfaced.

Thankfully, the plots ahead thickened, and for a time, he managed to ease the tension from his muscles. But as was inevitable, he again came to a widening. Weary now, he rested before going any farther.

He performed a cursory inspection of himself and his gear before settling in. A black sucker attached to the small of his ear soured his stomach. He didn't mind so much when they stuck to feet or legs, but the higher they climbed the more it bothered him. He pictured it wiggling into his ear and setting up its home in the tube therein and a sickness rolled into his stomach again. That image in his mind ruined his rest and he headed to the trail quicker than he should have.

He was midway through a ten-foot span when he suddenly lost his footing, nothing but mush and muck were under foot. Waist deep, he turned back, detouring to the far end of the plot he had deserted.

Hesitant now, he settled in for a long rest as he should have before, fearing he had stirred up too much activity nearby. He watched and listened. No slither, no hiss, no thump. His keen eyes searched the adjacent domicile. He saw no bedding areas, no dwelling mounds, and so he relaxed as he waited for his racing heart to slow and then proceeded on, cautiously.

An eight-foot stretch crossed, he paused again. The widening was getting steeper and steeper, and he wondered momentarily if it would be a good idea to turn away from this area. Instinct, however, told him to carry on. A voice said to him, "Go until you think you can't go any more, and then go just a little bit more…" He followed the voice's advice.

He followed the length of the house, trying to glean the

easiest crossing, and then finally finding what he thought to be it, he started out. He stepped with care and only when sure he would not find muck, and all the while, he begged his luck to hold out. "No slither, no bull," he told himself.

The residence he came upon was excessively limber. It tilted and warbled as he pressed his weight against it.

A ripple in the wet caused his heart to skip to a faster beat. He clawed and pulled, straining to pull himself up, fearing for feet with each fresh kick. He pushed off with the arbor as hard as he could, causing it to bow beneath his weight.

As something touched the toes on his left foot, Ray panicked. He shimmied up to the tuft of the dry, tucking his legs under his torso immediately, thrashing out with the stick as hard as he could into the wet, poking and retrieving again and again until he was confident nothing was near. Afterward, he curled up in a ball and soothed the rising and falling of his chest.

After what could have been only seconds, but seemed many long minutes, Ray rolled over onto his side, pressing his knee down as he went for support to gain his feet, standing uneasily. He took account of the toes on his left foot then, and finding five he sighed in relief.

Tall brush and weed-grass obscured his view and he had to press through its tangle to reach the other side. Making his way through such growth was tedious work and it took conscious effort on his part to resist the urge to push his way through it hastily. Using the staff as his guide, he laid aside bundle after bundle of weed-grass. Thick such as this could be a favored burrow of an Old Queen, and in such quarters, he did not want to meet her face to face.

Coming out of the tall, he jerked to a halt, amazed. Beyond the weed-grass and scatter brush was a hollow loch with its basin spread wide before him. He stooped down, making a low profile, blending in with the tall around him— such an open space frightened him.

The wet of the loch was clear and dark, readily deep. It abounded with ripples, and unfamiliar shapes darting here and there beneath its surface.

An uncountable mixture of groans greeted the mid-day sun, so many groans in fact that Ray could not even keep track of their bearing to him. As he surveyed the three arbor trees spread out around the loch, he knew without a doubt that he had finally come to the place lost and deep.

As he stood there, attentively watching, he saw a blunt, black, log-like head pass by in the waters in front of him. A moment later he saw a flash of the bull's yellow belly, the flailing of its tail. The bull smacked the surface three times, sank deep. Ray observed the spreading of the ripples in its wake. After a short passing, it surfaced.

He recognized Old Bull then as it lifted up from the wet

and trumpeted its arrival in the now-familiar baritone moan. He smiled as he heard the return greeting calls from the queens who were yet to mate. Old Bull had been late, but the queens had patiently waited. "Sorry," offered Ray as he watched Old Bull slip from sight again.

Ray sat back onto his haunches, mindful of his surroundings, and consequently flattening a small arch around himself. Several young bulls were exercising their rights, offering up challenges to Old Bull.

Ray watched Old Bull struggle with its first challenge as he set a warding ring about himself with four leaves of the stinging, urging the grizzled fellow on, craft and guile versus nimble and swift.

"Time's a wasting," Ray called out, realizing then that he wasn't afraid anymore. He had survived an encounter with a bull. He had found the place lost and deep. And he was one step closer to becoming a man.

Chapter Three:
Choosing

Old Bull successfully fended off challenger after challenger as Ray watched. While he was idle, he was not idle without intent. He was also searching through the ins and outs of the most prevalent question in his mind—the choosing. Which would he choose? The bull or the slither? It was this question that required most of his attention—the display was merely a diversion—but he still wasn't entirely sure of his choice. Both were excellent companions. Selecting one or the other as a companion would mean he would no longer be alone on his journey to manhood. The selection in itself would take him one step closer to being a man—if only he could choose.

He thought about the captive slithers and bulls in his village. No captive grew to the size they did as when they were free. That in itself seemed puzzling to him in this moment and while he was sure he had realized this before he found it odd. He also thought about Kotte and Emette who lost their companions. He thought about the sadness the loss brought to them and to the village. Kotte and Emette had both chosen bulls. They had both been a bit careless, granting their companions a bit more freedom than they should have, and allowing them to get a bit more of an appetite than was wise. *If he chose a bull would he be as careless as Kotte and Emette? Would he be able to be a strict master as was needed? Or would he be a bit too lax and bring sorrow to his people?*

Old Bull settled in with the first of his queens late in the day. The season was getting on though, and not many of the queens had waited as long as they should have, for which Ray was thankful, as it was already hatching time for the early broods.

Early was a good sign to him. He had been early, and in many things he had been the first and although this was mostly by virtue of the period of his birth, he exalted it all the same. Anything that peaked early was a good thing to him, and early broods were no exception. He saw a mother slither and a mindful litter pass his secreted place, tongues flapping, slit eyes staring. He held still until they were gone, not wanting to scare them into a frenzied evacuation.

"Don't worry, mother slither," Ray whispered to himself after the slither family had passed by, "I need one fresher."

He searched clumsily through his pack, removing all of its contents to get to the rounded hollow at the very bottom. The stretch of arbor was obtuse in shape, being about a foot long and gapped in the middle with one end sealed with heedful cross-stitching. The container had a small band on top that he could adjust for carrying and the backside was flattened so it would not roll when placed down. He admired his handiwork for a moment more, counting the days on both hands the container's making had required. Again asking himself, which would it be: slither or bull, and again, he did not know.

He considered his trek now, thinking that perhaps the choice lay obvious somewhere within it. He questioned the way the slither moved, gliding upon its belly. The bull had feet with which Ray knew it could race at tremendous speeds, even on the dry. The slither was graceful, the bull sometimes awkward. Yet the bull had clear advantages over the smaller slither.

Ray's eyes turned back to the loch. Old Bull was lethargically withdrawing as the day was nearing an end. As he watched Old Bull slip away, he searched the length of his staff with his hands. Every inch of the six foot, straight length was as familiar to him as his own hands. He had smoothed and refined its edges and strengthened it himself. The staff, like the container, was an integral part of his journey.

Thinking of the container brought back memories of Tall. Tall was his closest friend in the village. Tall was the one who helped him learn how to make the webbing on the end of the container when old three toes had declared that Ray was "unteachable."

"I made it, Tall," Ray said to the empty air, a sparkle in his eye. He imagined then that his lanky friend was smiling back at him. As he reclined back, his stomach rumbled and the thought of food and eating came to him suddenly. He decided it was time for a grand feast. He had found the place lost and deep—and he had done it on his own.

He took out a generous share of his gatherings, spilling over it a portion of the long sap he had secreted away. He did not portion out more than was needed, a drop here, two drops there, and not much more.

Ray shelved his anxieties for a while, until dusk arrived and the air turned cool and the humidity began to recede. Then reality began to settle in. Reaching the place lost and deep wasn't the goal—completing the rite of passage was. He must prepare himself. He must circle the three arbors, set his mark upon them. He must choose—and with thoughts of the choosing came doubt. *Is it true what the elders have said? Am I unteachable? Am I unworthy? Am I unready?*

Doubt led to hesitation. He waited perhaps longer than he should have, but he did manage to coax himself into preparing. He groomed himself, cleansing staff and body, flexing muscles. He made a large pile of cake-mud, intermixing wet and dry, applying it from toe to head.

In the last minutes of light, he took up the pieces of the stinging he had laid out, rubbing their oils over the hardened cake of the mud on his body. Staff and pack secured now, again he waited, eyes adjusting to the ever-increasing darkness.

Noting the homes, and those that lingered upon them, Ray purposefully set out, making cautious progress through the tall, skirting the edge of the deep. He still had not made his choice, rather he performed instinctively as he had been told.

He circled to the first arbor with confidence, setting his mark alongside the others: Ray son of Waddymarre, Third Village the mark said. Between the first and the second arbor was a thick with nests; Ray knew this, and he proceeded at a choked pace.

Weed-grass was all around him and though in other circumstances it could have served as camouflage, now it was a dangerous hindrance. He must rely only on his night senses, and the thrashing of his heart in his ears. He was afraid, but he turned his fear into his strength. He used it to shield him, to make him more aware of his surroundings.

Mentally, he tallied the number of nests he passed, noting the location of each. The silent guardians of the clutch were vicious and unremorseful in their attacks, and Ray knew that even a bull that wandered into their ward would not pass retaliation, yet he did not fear the guardian queens as much as he feared stumbling into another's stray lair. The slither did not always lie close to the wet and her nest could be settled anywhere, even atop the scatter brush he passed.

Halfway into a step forward, Ray froze, foot still hanging in the air. He waited, listening, was it the breeze, a fervent imagination, or was there something directly in front of him. "Is that you, Old Bull?" he whispered, the sound of his voice barely escaping his lips as the question flashed through his mind.

He backed up, paused again. He gleaned a hiss from the air, though not down low where he had expected it, perhaps level with his chest. He hesitated, breathed.

No, he corrected, in front of his face. The hiss came from in front of his face.

The gloom withstanding, he could have swore he saw a slither drawn up full, tongue lashing in and out, red eyes scrutinizing, and needless to say, he stopped, dead still. If the slither was real, if he wasn't imagining it, it would have to be the biggest slither he had encountered in all his life. Perhaps, it was Mother Slither herself, she who birthed all the slithers. If so, she was the greatest and most dangerous slither that ever lived—enormous. *Dangerous and enormous.*

His thoughts started moving in circles. He hesitated when maybe he should have pressed on.

Tiny flashes of hot circled around his face, lashed out at his shoulders, moved down his right arm. Had he been bitten? He was unsure. His thoughts were spinning. Everything seemed surreal.

Time clicked by. Reluctant to move, he continued to hesitate. Something touched his foot, he could feel it wiggling across now, dry and scaly. *Was his hesitation about to cost him his life or was it saving him? Was venom coursing through his veins? Was he about to die?*

He waited, fought to concentrate, to think. He breathed, slowly in and out, clearing his thoughts and calming his nerves as the smoot had taught him.

After what seemed an eternity, he took a hesitant step forward. The hot flashes passed. He proceeded on. The second arbor was not far off. He knew he could reach it—he told himself he could. "Quick of eye, quick of foot, quick of mind," he reminded himself.

Last season he had thought it would be so easy to find, to take, and to return, but then again, he had not understood the challenge. Anyone could find and take, and to return was as simple as following your path to its beginning. He understood this now, blood surging through veins, his awareness heightened, the senses reaching, reaching out.

He achieved the second arbor without further mishap and circled it he had the first. He was breathing hard now and a bit winded, but also excited. Within, he felt an inexplicable desire—a true need to succeed not just to prove himself to others, but to prove himself to himself. He was Ray, son of Waddymarre. He was not unteachable. He had learned all that he needed to become a man. He had taken no misstep—except well maybe that *one* but that one misstep was a lesson learned.

The elder's voice streamed through his mind. "You know which to take from Third to First, and so to Second, but which do you take from Second to Third?" He hadn't truly understood before but now the logic made sense. Before he had only considered the things he had known, the way from Third Village to First was known, but the elder had not been talking about Third Village, First Village, or even Second Village. He knew this now.

His night eyes saw the three villages gathered close; he was at First Village. The place between Second and Third was the deep, and therein the lost. He walked to the edge of the deep, kneeling down close to the wet, bringing a touch of it to his lips. The taste was almost sweet.

His step truer, his thoughts clearer, his senses keener, he

walked back to face the grand arbor, inscribing two simple markings along side the others: the sign for his name, Ray, and the sign that said he was Waddymarre's son. "One more," he hastened himself, adding, "Come on, Old Bull," as his sense of the grand game returned.

Almost on cue, a churning came to the loch, splashing, thrashing, a tangle; something must have gotten too close to an Old Queen. A bit more wary now and less driven by his elation, he hesitated until the echoes died. Mindful of step, knowing he had nearly succumbed to haste, he set out for the third arbor.

He passed the place where the convulsing, tiny ripples still licked the shore. "Don't worry, Old Queen, I don't want any of your litter," he quietly called out into the night, casting his druthers then and there. The choice was clear now; he had only to make it.

A prickly tangle barred his way, and just as Ray turned aside, he felt a familiar hot blast upon his flesh. Later he would not know what came over him, acting only on impulse, on instinct, he dropped down to hands and knees, the tiny puffs of air never straying, destined on his face.

He reached out with his right hand, while circling with his left, feeling a small twinge on the end of his nose at the same time. He grasped out with left and right, not quite convinced he was groping at empty air, yet not quite sure what to expect.

Slipping hands up dry, responsive scales, tightening under lower jaw with the thumb of his right hand, while clamping down with his left. The slither's first instinct was to coil, and it wrapped and wrapped, twining up Ray's arms until its tail crept round his neck, up under his Adam's apple, and clenched down like two giant hands upon his windpipe.

His thoughts spun wildly out of control and it was all he could do to keep from panicking. He fought with both hands as he tried to keep the slither's powerful mandibles closed, quickly discovering that the beast's head was twice as big as his own.

He knew then that he had stumbled upon the lair of a slither that was a queen of her kind—a slither that had stood the test of centuries and was as large as she was old. Struggle as he might, there was nothing he could do to ease the vise upon his neck and little he could do to keep the powerful jaws closed.

Primal fear overcame him and a primeval will to survive took over his every action. He hunkered down to his belly, rolled onto his back, the sudden adrenaline rush filling in where the long sap fell short.

He broke his left hand free, struggled to unwrap the tail from his neck while holding the powerful jaws in check, knowing he had only one chance to get rid of the angry mother, or she may have a pleasant feast waiting for the hatching.

Just before he released, throwing with all his might, it suddenly occurred to him that he didn't even know if the mother slither's nest contained hatchlings or eggs. *Was he about to stick his hand into a live nest? Was he about to make the last mistake of his life?*

He didn't hesitate. "Quick of mind, quick of eye, quick of hand," he told himself, as he released.

In the interim of the next few heartbeats, he lived his life in blurring explosions of images. While he wiggled his hand through the protective layers of the nest, holding one single breath, afraid if he let it go that he might never partake of another, he thought of all he had done, and all that could be yet ahead of him.

His fingers came upon a thing warm and leathery, several somethings warm and leathery. He cringed, the sour returning to his troubled innards. He exhaled; it was round and nearly ripe, but not yet hatched.

His hand passed over several, but he did not take one of the first he came upon. He probed onward, coming to one that was on the far side of the nest. Its surface against the palm of his hand felt warmer than any of the others, and this one, he plucked up, placing it immediately into the protective container he had made, delaying no longer.

The mother slither would be upon him any instant. He ran, forgetting better judgment, forgetting the dangers ahead, for the one behind was graver than anything he could imagine. He would have a new player in his game of chase and catch me if you can. He was sure of this. He ran and ran and ran as if his life depending on it—because it did.

He never came to that last arbor tree, not that night, and most probably not for the rest of his life, though if he had, he probably would have only jotted down one symbol, Ray, near the base of its trunk. Some events are life changing and life shaping—and he knew this now.

He had faced a challenge greater than any he had ever before faced in his young life and he had done so alone. He was no longer the son walking in his father's shadow. He was no longer Ray son of Waddymarre, Third Village. He was simply Ray and he now stood in a shadow of his own making.

The land beyond the hill beckoned strong now, and he willingly went. Perhaps following an imagined path back towards home would have been best, but he didn't heed those instincts. He knew the direction of the hill, and so he went, across a path he had never been before, yet he wasn't afraid. He carried on, head up, feet true, switching dexterously from house to house, pole in hand, precious cargo stowed.

Finally, he had become in his mind and through his deeds the thing he was always destined to be. No longer a child, he was a man now, at least as much a man as could be expected. He was after all only thirteen, having turned thirteen on his name day one turning of the moon ago.

Chapter Four:
Old Bull

In the twilight of day, Ray slumbered, an exhausting night passed. The filter between conscious and subconscious adhered to the phenomenon of the rising sun. He slept, eyes open, and in the window of his mind, he saw the sun rise, heard the night's sounds fade away and heralded the tendencies of the day. His weary body bade him to linger in rest a few hours more and so he did.

Awakening was more or less a switching from inward thought to outward thought. Ray made the transition willingly, but not easily. He stretched and craned sore muscles, arching back and molding it into place, cracking neck from side to side, massaging toes and feet, only then doing the inspection—the black sucker check—he should have conducted before his slumber.

Breakfast was moderate, and afterwards he collected handfuls of soft plumes from the weed-grass, sliding his precious cargo out of its holding, constructing a nest of sorts, putting the egg back into the container. "A slither," he said to himself, happy with his choice.

For a moment as he had held it, feeling its warmth in his hand, the outer layer had writhed and moved to his touch. The tiny one within was already beginning its struggle to break free from its prison home and Ray was pleased. He was hard pressed to resist the temptation to crack open the egg, knowing full and well this was not a thing he should do or even consider.

"Every thing has its time," he reminded himself, "Every thing has its time."

He thought about the tiny slither in the egg and it carried him through the rechecking of his pack and the stowing of his meager belongings. As he strapped on the pack though his thoughts turned inward. He thought of his experiences the night before. The change he felt within him but didn't see as he stared down at his reflected image in the nearby pool.

Not far off was a glade and beautiful lilies floated on the

open pool within it. In his world though, the In, he knew such beauty could be deceiving. The bright orange flowers grew only in places known as deep sinkings. Just below the surface of the pool was a muck so thick and deep that no one who entered ever escaped.

Suddenly he wondered if the lilies were a warning. *They were, weren't they?*

The other day he had seen the flash of orange just before the bull pulled him under. He felt an inexplicable urge to race back to his village. He began to rationalize his return. The only one who knew he had dreamt of the Out was the smoot and the smoot would never speak of it—it was forbidden to speak of another's vision quest. The villagers would see his prize, think him a man. He didn't have to continue. He didn't have to journey into the beyond. It would be his secret, the one thing he would never share with another.

He found himself saying aloud, "You know which to take from Third to First, and so to Second. ... You know which to take from Second to Third. You have placed your mark for all to see, for your children and their children to see. You have your life's companion. You can go home now, a man."

Everything felt right about what he said, except that the words rang hollow in his ears. *What did he really know? Was he really a man?*

He saw no change in his reflection, but he did feel

something inside of himself that he couldn't explain, that he couldn't rationalize away. He had set out to do what others before him hadn't. He had set out on the long path. He had set out knowing the journey to the place lost and deep was but one step of many. That thought alone used to terrify him. That thought alone kept him awake many nights. That thought alone isolated him even from his friends—friends with whom he couldn't share his vision and who wouldn't understand if he did. The village smoot hadn't understood it entirely either, so how could he or anyone else hope too?

He had shared some of it, however. Tall knew of the mountain and the wizard. Tall's paintings of the mountain and wizard had brought the elders. Perhaps everyone in his village knew of or had seen the paintings. It seemed now more likely than not. "My path is long," he whispered, near tears. He was still frightened by the sound of the words in his ears, but fear was a shield that brought him awareness and awareness made things clearer. He made his decision, cinched his pack tight, and then headed in the direction of the beyond.

When he started out, the sun was a large dome on the horizon, which was good for he had not slept as long as he thought he had. Somewhere ahead of him, he expected to find the widening that he had not found during the night, but with each new residence he crossed, the notion waned. The houses were drier here, they did not give as much as they ought, and this set him on edge. Thoughts played in the corners of his mind, images of the stone land and of the pale, ashen faces of those that dwelled therein.

Midday came and went, and still he did not stop. Sweat glistened off his darkened skin and dripped from his chin after running the course of his face. A large yawn issuing forth together with slow fire in his legs told him to rest, though he did not. A sense of urgency still prodded him along. He did not know how exacting the revenge of the slithers would be against him. A voice within argued that he had purposefully set them against him, and perhaps he had.

Mindful of his direction, Ray looked to the sun for guidance. He stopped, prodded his long staff into the wet, eyeing the far side, perhaps a six-foot jump. Ray backed up a step, checked the resistance of the domicile, and took a one-step leap, landing nicely an instant later. One less trip into the wet, he chided to himself. Ray grinned as he caught a glimpse of a low scrub not far off, and decided here would be a good place to rest.

After reclining into the small tree's modest shade, Ray eased aching joints and muscles. He rolled his guest from its confines and checked its progress. He felt the struggle strong in his hands.

He nibbled on light, dark, and bittersweet, the three being his favorites, attentive to the emptying of his pack, though there were several gatherings that he had not even considered eating. These were things that he had been instructed to collect, and not so much as he had wanted to, but rather because he knew it was necessary. Ray left the gritty and the stinging alone, pouring the remainder onto the surface beside him, sour weed, bitternut, black bark and black leave, and a few others, not mentioning of course those that he favored.

After making a mental note, Ray collected his belongings, untangled himself from the underside of the scrub and pushed on. Narrow avenues prolonged between the dwellings for a long stretch. Ray enjoyed this as he showed off his skill of foot, if only to himself. Careful calculations made, landing points checked, he would jump, feeling freer and bolder with each such leap.

"Watch me!" he called out, feeling renewed strength and excitement. Old Bull *was* watching, which Ray would have known if he had been paying closer attention.

Old Bull had secrets it wouldn't tell. It enjoyed a day's hunt better than most. Its long sojourn down, down and away from its home completed, it was on the return route now, not minding if it strayed a bit wayward of its course. It rended the wet with its tail, and slid up under an old log, raising eyes just enough so it could watch the youngster pass overhead, legs flailing in the air.

It was then that Old Bull slipped out of hiding, turning

wide, leaning back in with a graceful lethargy that it made particularly spectacular, and then watched again as the other passed by. Old Bull knew the boy's cargo, wizened on the seasons, it descried what the boy did not, a young one from a wee litter had been taken, revenge would be sweet.

Ray raced across another house, coming to the edge, nimbly crossing to the next. The area ahead widened, so he slowed, graduating from place to place with greater care. Scratching his head while regarding the sun, he contemplated his positioning, as he still had not come upon a neighborhood he knew. The night would arrive soon and again he would need a place to bed. Looking back, he guessed at his progress, the arbors long lost from sight. He ogled right and left, seeing no familiar dark pillars.

A journey into the wet at the next crossover could have cost Ray, but Old Bull was growing tired too. It would wait for the other to rest, and then it would find a suitable hollow, although a suitable meal would not be out of the question. It looked up at Ray shifting past, seeming to yawn as its jaws unshut. Perhaps it would dine on snap turtle or bog sucker, or perhaps not.

Ray beat his way through a mighty stand of weed-grass, observing as the seeds floated off or dropped from sight. He circumnavigated a stalwart bramble, checking for early offerings but finding only a few of last year's fruits rotted in their place with new buds only beginning to sprout.

He stopped suddenly, having found a wading, a secluded pool, centralized in the middle of the residence he occupied, fed by a legion of fresh flowings. A trickle of steam greeting the air told him it was a hot wading, not unlike those of his home village. The hot meant death to suckers and other pests, and as a rule, neither the slither nor the bull likened to the warm.

Ray jabbed and pecked all the same. When finally satisfied that it was unoccupied, he slowly slipped a foot in. The top skim of the pool was only a pale warm, but as he dipped deeper, soothing warmth caressed his foot.

The wading was just large enough for him to float across its face stretched long, yet only barely so. His pack and pole lay not far off, and he closed his eyes, relaxing. Curious about the depth, Ray reached for his staff, pushed it deep under the wet, as far as he could reach without finding a bottom. He didn't find this odd though. The hot wading in Second Village was over five times his height, or at least that is what he had been told—no one that he knew of had ever tested that premise; rather, it was accepted as fact. He slipped out of the wet momentarily, relieving his pack of a few leaves of the gritty, using this to cleanse himself in a peaceful frenzy.

Aloft the sky was delving into shades of gray and Ray decided here would be a pleasant place to spend the night. He could take another dip in the morning and be refreshed for the coming day. Arms spread eagle, legs out, he floated, the rush of bubbles streaming up, up under him, massaging away the stiffness. He rubbed the gritty into his scalp, along his arms, and around his privates. The new sense of clean satisfied him, not that he really minded being dirty, for how else could one travel, or hunt, or do anything else for that matter.

The Old Bull clambered up into a shaded glen not far away. It descried the cudgeling of the wet, the soft giggles and light song, falling away to its own affairs. With a string of powerful strokes, it launched from the hideout, eyes flaring, jaws tearing, shredding and mangling the captured prey. Belly satisfied for the time being, it slid back into the quiet spot and waited, lids slipping into place momentarily, jaws unhinged.

The night mischievously advanced from eve to dark, passing to the wee hours without much change. Ray slept in a relaxed style, eyes closed.

Old Bull, on the other hand, was awake and alert, and on the prowl. Its method of prowling was retarded though, it wasn't as quick as it used to be, not that speed mattered, stealth was the major advantage here and Old Bull had plenty to spare. It eyed the boy in the subtle dark from the far side of the steaming pool, inching its way closer and closer.

The air was cool as it swept past him, and Ray shivered in his sleep, moving into a closed ball beside the wading.

Absently, he scratched his foot. In his dream, he felt something wet shift across his leg and the scratching chased it away.

A twinge of pain in his side caused him to roll over. The ground was hard and unforgiving. His dreams were pleasant though, thoughts mostly of home. As his nose was plugged with mucus, he breathed in through his mouth, exhaling in gasps and moans, not feeling the tightening around his throat.

A myriad of sallow, listless faces crossed before his eyes. Off in the distance he saw the hill but behind him, the land was dry and gutted, lifeless. At first he thought the faces were of the Out, but then he recognized Tall's lanky drawn out countenance, sharp nose and deep-set eyes. *Deep-set eyes?* He asked himself. Tall didn't have deep-set eyes. *What was wrong?* He coughed and choked, stirring restlessly, coming to rest on his back.

Fighting to exhale a stifled breath, he wheezed and gagged. His eyes sprang open, meeting another pair of eyes that were luminescent red and descending upon him. Terrified thoughts siphoned into his mind. He turned his head to meet another pair of dark eyes and he heard a groan, a terrible deep sound—almost a growl. He staggered to his feet, falling, rolling and finally ending up in the hot wading. The creature round his neck flailed and fought harder, more desperately now. He heard a second splash, with a deeper, bolder resonance, and his eyes went wide.

Claws were raking at him while he held the thing before him; its head shifting ever closer, teeth flaring and dripping with saliva. Its twist round his neck tightened, making the extraction of each new breath harder and harder. He saw white flashes before his eyes, all faded to black, no air traveled in or out of his lungs, no sounds passed his ears, all the world froze. His eyes closed, all thought truly stopped.

Half in the pool, half out, his face in a stand of his own vomit, he awoke to find the world gray about him. His thoughts were still spinning, and his head ached tremendously. Sitting was an excruciating, painful ordeal, managed only through diligence. The first thing he saw was the overcast, frazzled sky and the next, that which had awoken him, a light downpour, which as he sat was growing full and heavy.

He did not attempt to move any further, nor did he seek cover. The rain pummeling down upon him seemed his return to life, and its touch the only sensation other than pain that he felt.

His legs were pillars of rampant scratches and gouges, his arms a mass of lacerations. Shock took over his thinking, and at first, he didn't realize what had happened. The bleeding was his first concern; he had to stop it. His first instinct was to the cake but the rain hampered the application. He began the long climb to his feet, ready to flee, to run as fast as he could to somewhere safe, realizing only then he didn't know where that was.

A thing black and lurking caught his eye, as it bobbed about the small pool, and without thinking, he reached out and pulled it towards him. The thing was thick and slimy, an empty stalk oozing at the end he had grabbed. Only as he flung it away did he espy that it had once been a slither. He was baffled now, vividly recalling the bull attacking him, raking him repeatedly with its claws, teeth flashing, jaws snapping.

He trembled. He would have closed his eyes, sliding into a catatonic slumber, if he hadn't heard a distinct sound far off blending with the thick fall of the rain. It sounded like the blowing of a great horn, or as he likened it to the call of Tall's flitter flute.

No longer slumped over near death's door, he felt a surge of strength and clarity of mind, his belongings not far off had what he needed, a short-term remedy to be sure but a temporary remedy was better than none. The container of long sap was there as he knew it would be, and he squeezed with both hands, letting the liquid run and slip across his tongue. Soon afterward, everything began to spin. He tumbled to his knees, collapsing beside his pack.

A watchful Old Bull, not far off, slipped back into its hollow.

Chapter Five:
Land Beyond the Hill

A tempestuous sky looked on as Ray slept, fading from violent black to passive gray. He awoke beneath this sky, not knowing whether it was day, night, or somewhere in between. He applied the cake-mud in grand doses, cringing as he did so, but telling himself it would eventually ease the stinging and prevent infestation. All the while, in the back of his mind, his only thought was the realization of whose eyes he had seen in the dream—the wizard's.

He took a deep breath, latched onto his staff, using it to

help him to his feet and once there, discovering that most of the pain and fatigue were gone. He crouched to his knees, leaning down carefully to get a small, unstoppered container, cursing as he did so. The long sap had been a precious gift and now it was gone. Nevertheless, he plugged the container's top and dropped it into his bag.

Low banks of fog made progress arduous, but he crept on. This day the fog was not as big a hindrance as his weakened condition.

Hours passed, a fair distance traveled, he decided that he wasn't really feeling all that poorly considering all that had happened, or could have happened. Lunch was a long, drawn-out affair that he should have never sat down to eat; the ground felt so soft, and the climb to his feet so far, though he eventually continued on.

His path growing further into obscurity, he picked his way with increasing care. Travel during the encroaching night would be out of the question and that suited him just fine. He managed step after step, working up to a rhythmic speed.

Rain returned as a fine mist, later turning to a light drizzle. His mood turned increasingly pensive and somber with the changing weather. A gray world made gray thoughts.

The stone land seemed so desperately far away and everywhere before him, he imagined he saw the white, white faces of the Out. But it was the one face that frightened him more than any other. The face with the deep set eyes, the face of the wizard.

Behind him, sometimes he thought he could hear voices, or make out dark shapes shifting about. Once he thought he had heard Tall's voice, though he couldn't be sure. In a sense, his own voice was telling him that home was behind and nothing was ahead, and while he wanted to listen to the voice, he couldn't.

An image whirred before his eyes, the foreboding hill, rising up from his lowland home. "The land does not shift, nor quake, not even a tremble," a voice whispered to him, "It is torrid, staunch and dead."

Ray stopped, checked his course, momentarily catching a glimpse of a pale, fiery ball in the sky. He snapped out of his reverie. Afternoon, he reminded himself. He crossed over to the next dwelling with care, making a short leap.

After bypassing a mixing of byways, he began to look for a place to spend the night. Near exhaustion, he could not go on, nor would the light permit him to go on much farther. Using small steps, he trudged along his chosen path, the imaginary line between nowhere and somewhere.

The night would not be all bad; the drizzle had ceased its irritation. He wouldn't find out for some hours that something special had chanced during his amblings this day, though it would upset him when he did.

Evening did not sweep in as it had the previous nights. It was more of a slow, gradual takeover from gray to black. Gray attempted to take a few steps back near the end, but the darker hue eventually won out, and night arrived. He found himself still on the move, and not wholly prepared to stop. His eyes had been ever adjusting to the trivial changes, and so for a while he had not noticed the arrival of night. It was the absence of change that aroused him to the fact, not the change itself.

The mist persisted, rising mostly from the wet in thick, billowy clouds, prodded into movement by small puffs of air that one could not call a wind since it really wasn't blowing in any particular direction or with strength of purpose. Standing on a moist ledge, a twinge of pain came to him, first in his toes, and then up his foot.

Another time he would have cast it off, since his body was already fatigued and troubled by a number of small aches and pains, but the fog irritated him, and so he kicked out with his foot, stomped down. His foot came down on something slippery and slimy.

A whisper in his mind said, "Black sucker, Black sucker." The bile in his mouth suddenly became abhorrence as his stomach soured. He despised suckers, large or small, it didn't really matter, though the large ones were more dangerous, and the small more bothersome.

He maintained his retreat until he reached the center of the house where he set up camp for the night. It was during this preparation that he discovered something else. The small arbor encasement stirred with fresh life; the shell was broken.

He would not find rest as soon as he had wanted, though he was bold enough to hope that when the ordeal was ended he would be able to rest sounder and safer. Two tiny balls of pale red stared at him from the other side of the meshing on the container's top.

He was overjoyed, though he wasn't sure if his friend was completely out of the shell, or if only the head was free. He watched and waited, and the miracle unfolded to him in tiny sounds and pulsations from within the container.

He hadn't expected this time to come for several days. He had not even cleansed his mind or performed any of the normal ritualistic preparations. He had been too caught up in his own affairs and now something that would affect the whole of his life and the scope of his journey had unfolded without him.

He was on the outside looking in. His face was pressed so close to the mesh that when the unexpected flicker of tongue touched his nose, he cried out, startling the little slither, and sending it racing away into the shadows.

"I'm sorry. It won't happen again," Ray whispered, and though it seemed he was talking to himself he carried on,

"Come on, you can come back. I'm not going to hurt you."

Turning a cupped hand up, he released the latch on the container's meshed top. A flood of the elder's words flowed through his mind as he did this. "The first moments of meeting are the most important. First impression is the lasting impression. Be true to your intentions, and voice them to him, and if he is willing, he will accompany you, and if not, he will turn away."

Before his eyes, images of all he had endured to get to this point raced, emotions sweeping across his face and playing with the pounding of his heart. He looked ahead now, as far as he dared to reach. "When it is over, you will be free, if it is your wish," he whispered as his thoughts raced on, not lingering long on that one rationalization. He closed his eyes and pleaded.

The tiny slither had his wits about him. The calling of the wet and freedom beckoned, and he crawled across his hand, flopping onto the refreshing, wet ground. It did not stop there, though it hesitated briefly. He did not know this; he only knew it was gone. Fearing he might accidentally squash it, he froze in place for a long time, finally crouching down to his haunches, where sleep would later find him.

A clear day came but he did not welcome it. Finding himself alone, he wallowed in self-pity. A late start allowed the last remnants of the haze to burn off. Food was tasteless as it passed his palate. He ate for subsistence, nothing more. He came to the edge of the wet, closely viewing its every nuance: a ripple, a wave, a branch or twig floating past.

He considered his quest at an end. He would find no new love, no new bond, for his realm, only remorse and perhaps in the end disdain. The connecting link had been severed before it had begun and he had no one to blame but himself, and this was a momentous burden for him to carry.

At that moment, the instant where he considered turning back and running home, which he could have done easily though the consequences would have been severe, a voice whispered in his thoughts, "Go until you think you can't go any more, and then go just a little bit more…"

He gazed at the rising sun, into the wide space highlighted by its passing, realizing then that he did not want to turn back. He wanted to go on, to go on until he could not go on any more. He couldn't have known that at that moment, tucked within the shadows of its new home, the tiny slither waited. No, he had made his decision independent of this, and it was something that would stick in his mind for a long, long time to come.

The previous day's precipitation, not at all uncommon, had made the residences wet and slick, and everything he brushed against irritated him. He trudged through thick mud, hard slippery rock, and through the wet itself, in unceasing repetition. It was during this, some hours later, that he found himself sinking in wet and muck up past his knees, balancing himself with his staff, and trying to pull himself out with little fortune.

Even before starting into the crossing, he had seen Old Bull lounging on a large, dry rock. And there Ray stood, stuck, sinking, but Old Bull, somewhat cocked off to one side of the large, protruding boulder, didn't budge, and Ray would never know why.

At about waist height, Ray stopped sinking into the muck, and now the only question that remained was how he would break free. With his walking stick, he tested the depth around him, driving it down and prying it out afterward. He could try to back out, but that wouldn't necessarily solve his problem.

He slipped the pack off his shoulders, allowing it to float free and luckily the seals held or it would have sunk straight to the bottom and disappeared. Still, he made enough noise that he didn't hear the bull's careful slip from the rock and he panicked a moment later when he noticed the emptiness. His wild thrashing only worked him deeper into the muck.

Re-collecting thought, he tested his weight against the pack, utilizing leverage from his staff, though he did not lift far, and as soon as the leverage waned, he sank back down to where he had begun. He twisted right, bending back, scanning the surface, probing with his stick, did the same to the left.

Off to his right was a partially submerged trunk, blackened and ripened by the wet, yet it was just beyond arm's reach.

Hearing no sounds of movement nearby, and alarmed by this silence, he returned to frantic engagement. Eventually, he worked one leg free, but as it became unglued he toppled over, finding himself gargling the murky substances he had been churning up. Arms flailing, legs kicking, staff in one hand, pushing the pack in the other and using it for ballast, he scrambled, giving it his all.

Old Bull looked on from a new vantage point, mostly oblivious to the hand that stroked its oblong head and whispered things it understood but barely so. Bathing in the bright, warm sunshine, satisfied with the fledgling's crossing, it closed its eyes, scratching with absent direction at the moistened earth beneath it. It would wait for a while longer before pushing on its way.

Ray brushed himself down, cleaning away most of the muck with a bit of grit, making for the low rounding he gleaned in the distance. He had not recognized Old Bull, nor seen the grizzled, timeworn elder stroking the bull's head. This was just as well, as Ray wouldn't have understood.

Ray sucked in at the air, fighting a burning weariness. He knew better than to persist in respite, but he did not heed this knowledge. He lunched early and ate more than he should have, reworking the cake-mud when he had finished and leaving himself a reminder that he needed to collect more supplies: two pieces of weed-grass, the thick, limber tufts from down near the root, which he tied around his left wrist.

He leaned heavily on his staff as he surveyed the distance and the close. "One step at a time," offered a whisper in a melancholy tone. Ray took a laden step forward, and thus he continued on his way. The stone land beckoned. My path is long, he thought, considering the weight of the words upon him. He did not jump, nor skip, nor did he take joy in the sense of the hunt; he simply moved on.

The avenues he ambled across, shifting from house to house, faded rapidly away from memory and sight. It was under a mid-afternoon sun that he descried a low scrub not far off and he wrestled with an undeniable yearning to stop for the day. He knew he could rest there in the scrub's shade and watch the night pull in. The temptation grew until it took a conscious effort to maintain his pace as he crossed the residence.

He dropped the pack from his shoulder in front of the scrub, slumping down to his knees, mindful of the waiting shade. He slipped the seal, delving inside the pack until he came upon a dark, round leaf.

Skillfully, he divided the leaf into two pieces, slipping one into his mouth between cheek and gum, and the other he sacrificed to the shade. He lingered no longer, however. He hated the pasty taste of the black leaf and so he could envy without regret.

A partial grimace touched his countenance as he came to a new house. He recalled with distinction a day Ephramme and Keene had been selected and not him and Tall. Tall had been the one to slip the half leaf into their packs, claiming a piece for himself and giving Ray the other.

Ray didn't understand at first, though later he had. He wondered how long he could keep the paste at the side of his cheek this time, thus holding his muse. Tall had also been the one that had told him to take the black nut, though Ray still saw no use for it.

A childhood rhyme came to mind. "Scatter bush and weed-grass blowing in the wind. Scatter bush and weed-grass shaking in the rain. Scatter bush and weed-grass sticking through it all." Ray chuckled to himself, hearing the mild, playful voice of his mother in his ear, more memories of the past. He repeated the words now from the rest of the rhyme, softly aloud as he walked. "The tall, the thick, the wide, the deep, in and around, out and in, out and around, scatter bush and weed-grass," there were more lines, and though he knew them all, he stopped. He was mindful of his step again, and that which was around him.

The playful thoughts didn't stop the weariness from setting through him sooner than he would have hoped, and after venturing across a second widening, one neighborhood farther along his path, he called it a full day. His body demanded rest, regardless of the lingering light above, and heedless of the paste on cheek and gum. He did not find such a comfortable spot as he had passed up, yet he did not care. Immediately after laying stinging to ground, he went to sleep, and many dreams played out and in before his unhindered eyes.

Chapter Six:
Watching at the Edge

Ray greeted early morning thinly and coldly, and several hours of travel did not improve his demeanor. He found no limberness in limbs, no skill of feet this day. He simply plodded on. An empty dream just before awakening had left him feeling lost and alone, and as he contemplated his surroundings he knew this to be true.

He was not part way or mid way along the stretch from Third Village to Second as he had sought to hope; he was passing along and through places he had never been, and as far as he knew no one had ever been.

Scattered clouds overhead followed him throughout the morning, though he paid them no heed. High day came, though he did not care.

Sweat trickled from his furrowed brow, his sores itched and burned, making him want to scratch them at every turn, and somewhere along the path he had lost his covers, so now he trudged upon bare feet. This day he had meant to do some gathering, yet so far he had not, and so this was what he set his concentrations upon with the coming of afternoon. His list was long. He needed to gather the dark and the light, the bitter and the sweet, and of course the gritty.

The rough, low bush, the gritty, was the easiest to find, for he knew the type of abode it favored, yet it was not the first bush he came upon. The first he found was low, yet wiry, and he snatched up its slender branches, taking even more than he should have, and this seemed to appease his disposition somewhat. He worked in an arching circle, outward from his find, searching for the other things on his list, and thus he passed the time until dusk.

During the time of twilight, he continued his pursuit, while also seeking a not so somber locale to pass the darkness in. A hot wading, he thought, what he wouldn't give for one to soothe his troubled soul and weary body in. He settled for a low scrub, though its warding shade was not as pleasant as it would have been in the day. He still had a lingering taste in his mouth, which he spit out. He ate absent of taste, reminiscing, placing the small of his back against the thin trunk of the scrub.

A few strands of the day's light lingered and he seized the time to fiddle with his pack, organizing its contents from top to bottom. He came upon the arbor tube and placed it on the ground with pained airs, for it represented something he could not have.

He tore a leaf of the black in two and placed one in his mouth and the other he slipped in the small holes of the mesh. The pasty sampling on cheek and gum accompanied him as he slept.

Molested by vivid, pointed renderings, he awoke before the day. He had felt things crawling on his hands and face, up his back, along his arms and legs, despite the ward he had provided. His thoughts swirled and swirled, and in his deepest dreams he saw the eyes—the eyes of the wizard towering over him as he climbed and clung to the rock.

Hurriedly he inspected his skin from head to toe, expecting to find a legion of suckers, though he found none. It was with the first pink-orange branches of the new day's sun that he saw the tiny creature nestled beside him, seemingly taking of the warmth his body provided.

He was stunned as tiny eyes sprang open and a small

tongue flitted in and out of a mouth. Holding his breath, he held out his hand, palm turned out, and to his utter delight, the baby slither crawled up into it, accepting his offer.

Awestruck, he sat motionless, yet his heart thumped wildly. Dawn came; morning passed. Ray did not notice and later he would not be able to recall a single moment of the hours that ensued from finding to choice to movement. Steadfast, able feet carried him onward. He placed his walking stick with distinction, walking without pain and without worries.

He fumbled through a list of names he had fancied before setting out. Keene had been the one that had told him he must name his new companion and so he stopped every now and again to whisper a name into the small cage.

The little slither had not responded to any of the names and he was getting flustered, that is until he forgot the names he had learned, leaning towards inclination. "I will call you True," he called out, which as he said it, face against the mesh, earned the first response.

"True, it is," he re-invoked.

A low murmur from his stomach spoke of his negligence to himself. He released the latch on the cage, no longer afraid that True would slip away from him. He delved into his sack, relieving it of a full dark root and a full light, one piece of sour weed and a bitter nut—his celebration feast.

He was unsure if he could eat it all, but he was sure going to try. He spread his banquet onto the top of the pack with care and began working his way from left to right, nibbling on a piece of this, mixing it down with a bit of that.

Hesitantly, he turned his eyes away from his meal, feeling a longing presence upon him. Until that moment, he had had only thoughts for the food before him. Now he saw the flashing tongue and large, piercing stare fixed on him. He sensed longing and hunger, understood his blunder of etiquette.

He offered the tiny slither a chunk of the light, but True only turned away from it; a piece of dark received a similar rebuttal. "What do you want?" Ray asked, "Will you eat this?" He had a bit of sour weed. True turned a full circle, and sprang away towards the wet.

He panicked, chasing after his small companion, nearly stepping on it in his haste. Ray froze in place, examining the ground beneath him. "TRUE?" he called out, hearing a tiny splash nearby.

He scrambled to the edge of the wet, galloping in huge pacing strokes. "True, are you still there? Don't leave me!"

He waited, struggling with a myriad of rampant thoughts. "I didn't know!" he added in a whimper.

Something slick and wet crossed his foot, and he shrieked. His first instinct was to smash down with the opposite foot, yet he did not and this was a good thing as True was sitting on his foot, tongue flashing, eyes nearly closed.

He walked back to his spot, the low scrub not far off, carefully tendering his bantam friend. With soft fingers, he dropped True into the comforts of the nest, picking up his pack, sliding the thin strap attached to the cage over his shoulder. He adjusted the strap so the tube was propped directly under his arm. True would ride beside him, with a full view.

A late outset would mean a late stop for lunch, so he kept the foodstuffs he hadn't finished handy. He paused at the edge of the wet to gather a few handfuls of its preciousness and with thirst quenched, it was time to move on. He found purpose of foot and direction; his spirits were high and his thoughts lofty, all because of a minuscule creature, no bigger than his pinkie stretched out full.

Just after passing across to the adjacent dwelling, he coughed out into the silence, "Where are you, Old Bull? The day is young. Come help me on my way!"

Anxious feet could delay no longer, and with them, he swept away. The feeling of sport had returned; the hunt was on. A warning groan breaking the air startled him and set his mind to frenzied reaction. He was running, racing; his elation peaked.

He had indeed stumbled onto a residence that was

occupied. The bull was swift, but Ray was swifter. The bull was crafty and wise, yet Ray had the advantages of youth. He plunged into the wet with the bull just seconds behind him, though he did not have to look back to know this.

His jubilation soared as he met the dry, racing over the small plot, thundering into the wet once more. Now he was unsure if the other still followed, although he hoped the bull did, for he did not slacken his pace. "Catch me, catch me if you can!" he taunted.

Hesitantly, he slowed after crossing several avenues, plopping a large piece of the bittersweet into his mouth, and only then as he turned eyes back out to his surroundings did he realize what was ahead. The dead land rose up before him and he feared its touch and its approach—the touch of mourning, the touch upon land which was not his own.

Behind him, a thin arm toted a firm hand, waving it back and forth, before rounded shoulders and unsteady legs carried the wizened figure away, though Ray only looked ahead and didn't see this. Old Bull slipped off the lackluster log it had adjourned upon, lazily following the retreating figure.

Eyes fixed straight ahead, never veering, he pressed on, those last few blocks seemed to last an agonizing eternity. Unrestrained considerations ripped through his mind, he would race up to it and plunge headlong onto its tracks. Except the closer the dark stone loomed, the more his determination waned. The hill grew before him. He could not see beyond it. He could only see the gradual slope lifting away into the distance.

He did look right and left now, studying the long gray line he approached. A hunch bade him to take True from his cage. "Look!" he said, "Look what awaits us!" True slipped around his palm in close circles and then made for open spaces, in particular, the wet. Instinct told the slither it was hungry and where to find its next meal. He watched it go, this time without fear or anxiety, waiting patiently for the tiny creature to return.

He abided at the fringe of the wet fearing to breach its limits, wasting the day until it spilled over into late afternoon. The dead land was beyond and he saw it dark and hard before him. Curious, he had ventured to touch its face once, and only once, and now he vividly recollected its unyielding hand upon him as he urged the last of his shivers away.

Thinking he heard something, he slunk down to his knees, blending into the greenery. He never took his eyes off the stoic, gray face of the upgrade, the brink of the land beyond the hill.

His quick-witted response was not without reward as heavy footfalls against the hardened stone grew audibly closer. He sank to his haunches, exhaling in guarded breaths, carefully removing his pack and slipping it beside him. A tremor erupted across his face as a pale, thick legged figure approached. He twisted his cheek between his uppers and lowers and bit down hard. The outsider had come to the edge of the wet and touched his hand to it, drinking of it.

Another shiver passed as he perceived the ill probe of the other's eyes. Ray saw the face clear now as the other stood there at the edge. The face was long and pulled taunt. The eyes were brown—weren't they? "No, that's not right," he told himself.

The sun caught the other's eyes now as the man turned to look over his shoulder momentarily. The eyes were blue—light blue—and the hair fair and long. The man was outfitted in a dark tanned suit, obviously thick and cumbersome, as lavish beads of perspiration dripped down his face. On the man's feet and hands were similar coverings, more things that made Ray uneasy. But the thing that made him the most easy was the sign stitched onto the breast of the suit. It was unmistakably the staff of the wizard with a lightning bolt shooting out of the glowing crest.

A wave of the arm brought others to the brink of the wet. They toted large canisters that they began to fill quickly. Ray gasped. The outsiders were stealing from his home.

His first urge was to jump from his concealment and chase them away. Then he saw more come and these men bore things that flashed in the light and in their hands, long and sharp. They stood with wary, angry eyes.

A third group came and now the outsiders did not stop at the edge. They pushed into Ray's precious wet, beating at the undergrowth and plowing through it like unthinking beasts.

Ray curled up into a close ball, pulling his pack closer, shifting into fuller cover, his eyes never wavering far from those that approached. He gulped for air as they passed precariously close. He wanted to scream at them, "What do you want? Go away! Leave my home!"

A smile, sly and swift, passed his lips as he saw a dark shape in the water easing closer. He saw the eyes and tail, but he was sure the others did not. He was praying for them to come closer and receive a bit of repayment, not realizing that what he wished for was wrong.

He heard a cry and saw the lash of tail and teeth, and he screamed a voiceless "YES!" But the hope died quickly. Those of the Out descended upon the large bull with quick precision. The outsiders hacked and thrashed at the wet, running after the bull as if it was a game and all the while, ignoring the pleas of their wounded compatriots as one by one the bull sank its teeth into their flesh.

After dispatching the last of the group, the bull sank deep, dragging the last of the outsiders to fall with him. The bull would have its feast. Ray invoked a second voiceless cry of elation. He chose that moment to slip away, moving farther away from the outsiders, deep into a thick stand of weed grass where he would never be found.

His heart still pounding in his ears, he breathed a sigh of relief. He chastised himself for his foolishness. He never should have stayed so close. He should have slipped away as soon as he heard the outsiders approaching. The Out was a dangerous place; it was the wizard's domain. He knew this. *Why had he stayed? Did he really believe the stories that outsiders drank dirt? Did he really believe the lord of the heavens made the wet for his people alone?*

His thoughts scattered as the large outsider, the one that had arrived first, charged the bull as it re-surfaced, diving recklessly into the wet, directly on top of the bull. The waters churned suddenly and violently as the bull and outsider struggled. The other outsiders began chanting, "Braddick, Braddick," and Ray could only surmise that this was the outsiders name.

Ray saw a tangle of tail, teeth and legs, and then all became red. The struggle subsided. Braddick's body floated to the surface and then the yellow underside of the bull floated to the surface. Ray recoiled as he realized the bull wasn't just any bull—it was Old Bull.

The outsiders were quick to pull Braddick out. As Ray watched, they pressed upon Braddick again and again until he coughed and choked and spat water. Then Braddick did the strangest thing Ray had ever seen, he raised the stump of his right arm and cried out. Yes, the roaring voice was touched with pain. But more jarringly it was touched with glee as well, almost as if the missing hand was a sacrifice and the stump of the arm was a prize.

Afterward Braddick and the others dragged the bull's carcass up to the dry and they did so with hearty cheers. Ray didn't watch what they did next, though he heard. In his mind, he pictured them carving the mighty bull and heard their rousing roar of cheers when the head was severed.

Ray opened his eyes for an instant then, and what he saw brought tears to his eyes. The head of Old Bull was propped onto the end of five long poles which were stick into the ground and though the carcass was gone, he could plainly see the blood-loss as it covered the dry. He fixed a defiant stare upon them, watching as they departed just as rapidly as they had arrived, carrying their trophy before them.

Ray's hatred of the outsiders grew several fold. Now he no longer wished to continue. There was nothing he wanted to see and nothing he hoped to gain. Before he knew what he was doing, he found himself rising to his knees and then he stood tall as it defying them to see him. It was his good fortune, however, to be so deep in the weed-grass that he was hidden from their view. Even if he somewhere down deep wanted to be seen and to share Old Bull's fate, the weed-grass shielded him from the outsiders' view.

He shouldered his pack, turned his back and walked away. The inner reflections of his heart and mind filled his vision. The Out, the dead land, was truly that: dead. Its people were without heart and feeling. No one of his kind would ever kill a bull for sport and he was sure the killing Old Bull was sport to these outsiders. It was one thing to defend oneself, quite another to seek out bulls and kill them as he imagined these outsiders did.

Chapter Seven:
In and Out / Out and In

Ray did not wander far before the darkness gathered him in. He welcomed the night sounds. The night was a time of solitude, a time to feel and to reflect. In his thoughts he mocked himself, "My path is long"; he no longer felt smug. He couldn't shake images of Old Bull and the probing eyes that were death, death to his dreams, and much more.

He sat still as a stout tree in a turbulent wind, contemplating images that spilled over into his thoughts. The bull had without a doubt sacrificed itself to save him.

He didn't know why or how he suddenly came to know this but he was sure it was the truth, and the realization was a powerful stroke of awareness across the plain of his mind's eye.

The stinging lay around him, though he did not feel its protective circle. In his heart, he mourned much more than loss alone. He had not retreated as far as he would have hoped, but instead, he had paralleled the stone land, following a jagged path between the In and the Out.

He wanted to turn away, but couldn't. It wasn't noble thoughts that brought him back or the wish to continue on, but preservation of his land and his home, thoughts of revenge. He wanted to make the outsiders pay for what they had done. In his eyes, he saw the head of the bull over and over, slumped lifeless, pierced through. If Braddick wanted prizes, Ray would give him a prize—one the outsider never bargained for.

Darkness did not mean sleep for Ray this night, not sleep in the true sense. He was idle, his eyes were open, and he could have been asleep by all other appearances, though it was his thoughts that kept him awake. It was an incessant, monotonous thought, from which there was no escape.

Countless hours drained away. He was oblivious to the passing, even oblivious to the minute flashes of heat against his face. True had slipped through the cage's door and ran back and forth under his chin, trying to gain his attention without luck. Ray was in his own realm though and it would take much more to break him from this state.

True was frightened and trying to warn Ray, and if Ray had been paying attention he would have known this. The man had come some hours after Ray had settled in, and he had not left.

True flashed his tongue again, adding to it a soft hiss. A harsh noise following this drove True back into frenzied prancing. Ray shifted uneasily, though he did not return from his reverie.

Images crossed before his eyes and voices, both familiar and unfamiliar. The visions frightened him while at the same time they attracted and lured him in. It was the same vision he had had back in the safety of Second Village, except now it had changed somehow, twisted, if that were possible. Yet throughout it all, the voice remained, urging him to continue and not to give up.

Morning found Ray as he found it. In the fading shadows of the night, he would venture to touch the land of death, crossing from In to Out with ease, but resisting the first crucial step from the world of the known to the world of the unknown. He walked with bowed legs and heavy feet, stepping harder and harder upon the unyielding surface. The firmer his placement, the firmer the land's rebuttal, and the pain in his legs grew. He found the lack of play, the lack of movement, uncanny and irritating.

In the stone land, there were no houses to cross, no avenues to come upon, only the bold face of the hill to traverse. Ray, however, was not yet feeling bold. He walked the sulking, mourning walk with fear and dread, staying near the edge. The rough, grinding face against his feet made him cringe with each new touch, and as soon as the shadows dissipated, he submitted to the need for safety—the need for the wet and the In.

He watched from hiding, crouching low in a weed-grass nest, or from a carefully selected thick, tracing the thin line of the border, not really knowing to where he went.

Night came and days passed, he watched and waited, venturing to the Out during times of shadow, returning to the In whenever panic necessitated. Many more times he watched as the outsiders came to the brink of the precious wet, though they were not all as fierce or as fearsome as those he first saw.

It was on the eve of yet another day, after a hasty gathering, a quick adventure, and a light supper, that he first saw her. She was the first of the Out that was not obviously male.

He had wandered long from the place he had begun and so he had no idea where he was in relation to his home, although the gray face of the hill was still before him. He watched with interest; that is, until she too stole from the wet. Curious though, he looked on as she filled only two small containers, pouring back a bit off the top.

This night he did not continue his roaming. He and True set up camp early, remaining where they were. The night lasted an eternity as he waited for day and then for afternoon, hoping she would return and not really knowing why. She was a thief like all the others; she took from his world, giving nothing in return.

He regarded True as he adjourned to the wait. His small friend was growing in surprising spurts. True was now almost a full hand in length, and along with the growth, grew the appetite.

True dined mostly on beetle bugs and other insects that Ray counted as bothersome, gathering them from the surface of the wet and usually swallowing them whole. A bond was forming between the two. Ray could sleep with eyes closed at night—sound, deep, healing sleep—knowing if danger loomed near True would find a way to wake him.

Ray had learned this that very first night. True's favorite time to nap was in the hot of the day. This suited Ray just fine. The two spent mornings and evenings together.

Ray had finally found a use for the black bark, which was naturally oily. He used it to rub into True's hide, thus easing the transformation of growth and renewal.

True was already shedding his initial coat and Ray helped to work it off. True's repayment was at gathering time as the slither instinctively learned to seek out the things Ray wanted. Ray was also acquiring an understanding of things True took an interest in, like fresh buzzers and flyers. And so, their partnership was forming.

As late afternoon arrived, the other returned, two burdensome buckets in hand. Ray crouched low, winding his way as close as he could get without fear of being seen. He studied her from foot to face, contemplating her allure to him.

Pale faces repulsed him, and the long, light hair he saw as useless and troublesome—and the outsider girl had a flow that swept down her back to the verge of her waist. Her eyes were different from the others Ray had seen, though. The eyes were blue, but not a light blue, rather a deep, dark cobalt that looked like two clear, clean wadings into which Ray could lose himself and his soul.

Ray watched her face as she filled the buckets, skimming off the excess. She had hollowed ridges, profound lines, stemming from nose to chin on the boundary of both left and right puffy cheeks. Lines that when she worked her face up into a slight scowl, gave her the resemblance of carrying an all-encompassing frown.

Lowered lips added to the excess of the etching, forming

the largest pout Ray had ever seen. For an instant though, her downtrodden grimace had blossomed into a full smile, and though it died as quickly as it had been born, upon later recollection Ray would come to call those lines laugh lines.

Sepulchral cast gave way to the premature arrival of night, a night Ray would not soon forget. He held True tight, the wind offered up the heavy scent of humidity to his nostrils and not far off lurked rain.

Ray glared with unwavering determination at the gray face of the stone land before him. He was going to venture out to it one more time; the thought of its touch upon him, however, slowed his sense of purpose.

Ray stood, shouldering his pack, regarding the rain's approach. It was almost as hesitant as he was to sweep forward, wanting to loom around him, circling right, turning back, but not coming directly at him. The first step was always the hardest and Ray knew this. He surveyed the edge for the shallowest crossing and upon discovery he gradually preceded on his way, though he never made it to the stone land.

Movement caught his eye, not far off a figure eased towards him. Ray had waited as the other had said, where he otherwise might have turned back. His thoughts had been hasty then, but not so now. He stood still, allowing the other to approach.

Ray was also confused—the smoot's visit was untimely

and unprecedented. *What was the meaning of it? Was his quest at an end? Had he failed? Worse yet, had he failed and everyone else knew about it? Why had he been told to wait?*

The venerable smoot seemed weathered to Ray. His eyes were laden with such a deep sense of pain, born in the wrinkles round eye and forehead. The wrinkles were time-worn centerpieces; Ray had seen several of them grow in his own time, however, the remainder appeared to have been chiseled into a stoic, granite precipice which Ray likened to the gray face of the stone land that he briefly turned back to look at.

The smoot was soft spoken and so Ray had to lend a close ear to the quietly invoked request to sit, reminding himself to remain attentive. He hated the way the other hastily tapped out instructions with the end of his stave: a quick series to listen up, once to the shoulder to sit up straight, once about the feet to watch their placement, a stroke to the left of cheek, to the right to fix eyes center—all things that Ray was currently enduring.

Ray sat up firm, eyes fixed upon a pair of weary obelisks, feet placed naturally yet guardedly, head raised, senses poised. He knew better than to speak first in such honored company, yet anxiety overpowered sense and he began what would become the longest and most remembered words of his entire life. The smoot made no gestures. Nor did he utter a word until Ray finished and even then, his sole response was a solitary nod. An elongated lull, anticipated, followed.

The smoot was not a hasty man and his words were never hastily offered nor hastily spent. During the interim that ensued, Ray cringed, biting upon his own tongue, reverberated words playing upon his ears. Then the smoot said in a time-softened voice, "I needn't tell you this, but I will."

Ray paid close attention, knowing the other said nothing without purpose. Ray crouched forward expecting a cataclysmic revelation.

"The answer to your question, your last question, is yes." The smoot stopped and smiled, a smile Ray had never seen before.

Suddenly Ray understood the jest, the first and only time the other had ever made light of any situation. Ray would quickly come to know the irony of it.

The smoot rapped Ray once in the knuckle for fidgeting and once on the shoulder to be mindful of his awareness. "How long will you linger before you admit the truth of your heart? Is it the stone land you fear or is it what you saw in your vision—the beyond?"

Ray didn't answer. He didn't have to, the smoot continued on his own accord electing to stop only to register the expressed response in Ray's eyes.

"You follow a path not unlike any of those that preceded

you. So what is it that you find so difficult that you have not yet gone on your way? The journey awaits. You must take your chance!"

"What about Old Bull and the outsiders?" Ray blurted out, holding back no longer, his face flushed with emotion and anticipation of rebuttal. "How many more of them are out there? And what will happen to me if they catch me? And do I really have to go? ... I have completed my path as far as I wish to go."

The smoot was silent, pausing seemingly until the last of the echoes died, speaking just when Ray set to sulking. "It was past time for my old friend. He was growing long of tooth, and would have gone soon anyway, as will I. We were much alike, he and I, ripened to the verge of spoiling. He always took to gallant performances though, so were different in that respect."

For a brief moment, the picture in Ray's mind was of a person, not of a beast.

"Our time is behind us, so we turned to look ahead and that is where you come in, Ray. You are ahead; you are the next link of our great arbor. Tall, Keene, Ephramme and Isaac will find culmination of their paths long before you to be sure..."

"But—"

"Don't look so surprised. I know the truth of your visions,

for there were similar aspirations before me, though I never reached my path's end."

Ray seized a breathing pause to interrupt again, "You didn't? Then I can turn back and everything will be right—"

"Not so readily. First, you must try." The smoot halted again, his eyes growing different, and Ray aspired to see a fondness growing beneath them though perhaps it could have been a misconception.

"But how will I know when I have done all that I can and it is time to come home?" asked Ray.

"You will know, just as I knew. Tomorrow, she will come early and you will have a choice to make…"

"She?" inquired Ray.

The smoot glared at him and Ray provoked no further inquiry. "And so you will endeavor upon the next step of your journey, if it is your choosing." He stopped again, slipping something into Ray's hands, a small circlet of orange flowers carefully preserved—the same orange flowers that stood guard over the deep sinkings. "Add this to your bag, and with it, you will remember your home. Now, it is time I went about my way…"

"But it is dark, you could remain here with me this night," Ray said. "In the dark you could lose your way."

"I have walked the ins and outs of this neighborhood many, many times"—a hint of emphasis on ins and outs—"you are remanded to think only of yourself." The smoot stood, preparing to turn away, gathering up his staff skillfully in hand, adding, just before he turned away, "I wish you luck on the morrow, and hope you do indeed find the end of your path. You will be the better man for it."

"Man?"

"Yes, man. You are no longer a boy, Ray. It is two turnings of the moon since your thirteenth name day. You have passed the tests, and you are a man even if you cannot see this in your deepest self," and so saying the smoot turned and walked away.

Ray wanted to scream, "Is that it?" But he didn't say a word. He remained as was appropriate, watching until the other's form blended into the shadows.

Suddenly feeling exhausted, he allowed sleep to pull him in, and with True alongside him, he would have a pleasant night's rest. Somewhere in the hours of darkness he found peace. Peace of mind for himself, peace of mind for Old Bull. Peace that replaced bitterness; peace of mind that healed. Rain never found him that night, though a storm raged not far off.

Chapter Eight:
Return from Adalayia

The return from Adalayia passed without incident and for this Kerry was happy, and to prove this, she even ventured to hum her mother's favorite song "Calling to the Heavens." She stared out a window, recalling the city's sights.

It was not often she made the journey to the wizard's city—a thing she did more out of necessity than of desire, even though she enjoyed her time spent there. For her, there was no place like her own, simple home and her unworldly concerns. No hurt could find her here.

Life in the cities was rough, the wizard ruled with an iron

hand, and being of mild nature, she would not have survived long. She hated drudgery and tedious manual labor. She preferred to fend for herself in the country, for here she was the master of her own fate.

She owned no weapons and for this she was proud. Strife was far removed, her realm was at peace, a peace that had lasted for generations, and would last for generations to come. The barriers were not diffident edifice; they were purposefully withstanding. She knew this, just as she knew Stirling had succumbed one summer ago, which meant she was alone.

She wasn't frightened by the loneliness. She had made the journey on her own and it had chanced without mishap. She would make it again when the time came. She returned to her vigil upon the window, the day was ending, and as often was the case, this saddened her. After all, why did the night have to come at all, could it not always be day?

As the burning ball of the sun eventually fell from view, she turned away from the window. She checked the line of bolts upon the front door and the security of the windows, settling back in the rocker when all was finished—the rocker her mother had whittled away most nights in as did Kerry now.

For many long hours, she skipped back and forth, eyes upon the ceiling, knitting away time in absence. Sleep arrived somewhere in that time, though she could not be sure when.

Day came as a splash of color to a darkened land, struggling to break the horizon, meandering long, bursting upward. She was up and about by the time the sun was a full globe in the distant sky. Her morning routine was ingrained upon her just about as staunch as the land around her. Her dreams that night she would never recall.

Morning tidings were a mixture of offerings and collections, though she ate, as always, frugally. Afterward, she returned to the short, stout trees and eternally thanked them for their offering.

She admired their steadfastness, knowing they nurtured all they needed to sustain themselves from the very air about her. Still, her father had taught her and proven to her that to produce meat they needed what she provided, and so she was tied into their cycle of growth as much as they were tied into her own.

The tender meat of the fruit was a main staple for her and most of her people, and it was this that she traded in Adalayia, though it was dried and preserved for the journey by endearing hands.

The trees yielded variety, changing with the seasons, though she never felt poorly for exchanging their winter offerings for the things she needed from the city, primary amongst this being the white, powdery grit she knew to add sparingly to her gatherings to preserve and store them.

As she wandered from tree to tree greeting them, her stare ambled out into the hard that surrounded her hovel. Momentary reflections went out to the stone crossing, the vast, steep bridge that separated the Adalayian proper and lead to the capital city of Adalayia.

Thinking of the city made her think of Stirling, sad thoughts for a heavy day. Heavy because the sense of loneliness had returned once more. She broke the silence with a piercing whistle, a high-pitched whine formed from a spout of air into properly cupped hands.

Kerry thumped the top of her father's crossed rod, waiting impatiently now, tossing another ensuing toot into the air, turning away disappointed at long last. She returned to her chores—self-implemented labor that perhaps didn't need to be done at all—throwing surreptitious glances upward.

"Off again," she whispered to herself, angrily.

She swept out her house, cleansing it of dust and soot, chasing away lines from the windowsills and billowy plumes from the rafters. She made up the bed—a bed she had not slept in for some years now. Gathered chairs, three, around the small, cylindrical table tucked into one end of the small structure.

A line of sweat broke her brow and this pleased her. She aimed the rocker towards the window at such an angle that she could watch the sun wander through the sky throughout the day and then easily turn to watch the sunset. Afterward, she moved back outside, beneath a benevolent sky.

She greeted the trees again, reassuring them, tidying away their woes, waiting until precisely midday to touch a bit of life fluid to their limbs. She whispered words as she poured, words her mother had passed down to her through the years and words that had been passed down to her mother and her mother's mother and so on through the ages back to the dawn of Adalayia. Three times a day, she spoke thus, granting only as much as she needed to receive in return what she wanted.

Upon finishing, she emitted a shrill summons to the heavens again, and again the call went unanswered. Her thoughts were troubled now, where had the other gone?

She called out again, anticipating an answering return that did not come. She did not fear the other's passing though. A gift had been placed before her stoop that morn and she had properly dressed it out, relinquishing a full half, part of the bargain, cleaned and waiting. A shiver passed along her spine and she returned indoors.

Deep thought carried her back to the top of the stone bridge, staring down as she had that very first crossing into the endless falling off. She recollected now that only the sight of Adalayia had coaxed the fears from her heart. She would have moved to Adalayia then without ever returning home had her father not pleaded with her to change her mind to the contrary. Her promise could not keep away her yearnings though, and thus the heavy thoughts that she began the day with remained with her throughout the day.

Shifting in endless strides back and forth, she waited, adhering to the settling of the sauntering sun. She dispersed the last of the life liquid and then began the long trek to the water's edge.

The long walk didn't bother Kerry; this was a time for easing the tensions of the day. She meandered around each falling off, making her way gradually downward. She had taken this stroll a thousand times with Stirling, and many thousands more as three, but each time, she spied something new that she had not seen before and this made the journey worthwhile and in a way, magical.

New erosions of the land spoke to her. She understood the gentle outcroppings sprawled across the face of the earth, the way a sheer precipice reached up to lofty heights and the way the gently oscillating wind meandered between ridges and falling offs.

When Kerry reached the water's edge, she took only the meager supply that she needed, more come winter season, returning the excess, before she began the hike home. Returning home was more difficult than going as the trek was uphill and not down. She walked awkwardly then, levying the weight of the buckets, trudging uphill with strategically placed footing.

A fresh breeze rolled in just as she attained the summit and she paused to enjoy it, staring off into the sparse land. Her eyes followed a line that meandered to the edge of the horizon and she envisioned the nestled paths that lay secluded from sight, knowing most of them though she had never walked them.

Upon her return, she fancied a tremor of delight floating from tree to tree and for this she scolded them. "Not yet," she whispered.

The allure of the stone bridge was clambering upon her thoughts again. She passed through the doorway into her house, sealing the door, shifting to the window and settling into the rocking chair beside it. Weary of heart, she closed her eyes for a time, waiting for the arrival of the slumping sun. "Tomorrow," she whispered to herself for hopefully by then, she would have forgotten the things that brought her pain.

A lofty screech caught her attention and she shot from the chair, her eyes probing the empty crossed stave planted outside the door. The screech repeated and she sprang out the door, scouring the skies with hope-filled eyes. Into cupped hands, she replied, the whistle reaching far. The scream returned, but this time it was farther off as the other was going away and not toward.

She blew into her hands again, forming a perfectly shrill shriek. Again, the answering call grew more distant.

"Wicked, wicked, Waring!" she shouted. Stirling had bidden her to keep the beast sharp set, but she preferred to give it equally proportioned repayments.

She sounded off again, stouter and longer, louder than she should have. No call broke the air. She was frightened now, something drove the other off. She scrambled into the house in search of the lure. Sure it would bring the other home. She began slowly rotating the line of the lure, allowing it to slip outward a hand's length with each turning just as she had been shown and sure to allow it to flash against the sky.

She howled out with poised lips, not as fervid as her other call, but still purposeful. "Come back," she said in a half-spoken voice, "come back, I promise I will not go away again…"

The line was at full span now. Its thin, arcing shadow raced along the ground beside her. She offered whistle after whistle, turning the lure until her arm stung with pain.

Glumly, she returned to the vigil at the window, finding no pleasure in the spectacle before her. Dusk passed, night came. She still stared with fixed eyes, lost either in thought, remorse or remembrance. Tomorrow would be bright and beautiful, she promised herself.

Chapter Nine:
Strange Meeting

The smoot's visit had an impact on Ray though he was not entirely aware of the depth until he awoke the next morning and found a sense of peace and premonition. He ate breakfast while delving through another's eyes. True was off, finding his own meal near the brink of the wet, and amongst the scrub.

Admittedly persistent in his watch, he kept a close eye on the Out and while seemingly calm and collected by outward appearances, inside, his thoughts were turbulent.

He searched for hidden meaning he would not find so

readily, and beyond this, in the far reaches of his minds lurked shadowy remembrances. Temporarily his concerns went out to someone else, triggered by these far thoughts. Tall should have already arrived at the deep if he was as fortunate as Ray had been. Ray pondered what Tall's choice would be, wondering if it would be the same as his own choice.

A nearby rustling in the thick brought him back from reverie and his keen sight zeroed in on the small slither mixing through the bramble, coming to rest before him. He coaxed True back into the security of the cage, noticing the larger than normal bulge in the slither's belly. True was growing and so was the size of the captured prey. He smiled at the other's sluggish movement, knowing True would soon rest soundly until the hot passed.

Precious few seconds had passed, but by the time he looked back one of the Out had arrived, the girl with the laughing countenance, the one the smoot had said would come early this day. She had, and now he wondered what the choice he would have to make would be. True settled in, though Ray was now oblivious to this. He attended to the Out with earnest eyes, watching as the other filled the canisters resting on the ground before her.

He would not have seen the knobbed head if he had not been paying particular attention. The approaching bull was young and guileful, hardly stirring the surroundings as it lumbered towards its target. Ray watched with speculative interest, wondering which would be quicker this day. The other had already gathered her wares and would momentarily be safely on her way. He silently urged the bull to hasten, offering a sense of play to his thoughts.

He watched as the outsider girl surveyed her prize, preparing to depart. The agile bull slipped up to the very edge of the wet. "Beware lashing tail and gnashing teeth," Ray softly stated, his voice scarcely cutting the still air. He spied the eminent frown, as the other raised a canister to check its contents, ambling towards the wet to spill a portion back.

A breath seized in his throat, he almost cried out, "No, you're not supposed to do that!" The perception of play was gone in an instant. The girl was in real danger. Her sense of fair play in taking only what she needed was going to get her killed.

He watched the bull's tail sink; his heart skipped. The bull was about to make its attack. He watched as the jaws snapped upward, not even realizing that his feet were in motion until he was halfway between In and Out, and by then there was no stopping. The bull was a heartbeat away from the outsider girl, but which Ray had in his heart to deny it of a meal.

He slapped his arbor staff stiffly to the bull's snout and quickly wheeled around, half flying through the air, half flailing with his arms in a struggle to remain stable throughout his vaulting leap.

A trace of a smile crossed his lips as he landed squarely and cocked the bull on the head again. The bull was not as versed as Ray was, its instinctive tactic was to retreat, and though Ray knew the bull would at some later point have learned not to do this, the ploy worked for now. The young bull was not as skillful in the hunt as Ray was nimble.

Ray spun around catching a glimpse of the laughing face only for a fading instant. He followed the retreat of the bull, running wildly for cover and the sanctuary of his precious In.

He slipped his pack around his shoulders, rudely awaking True, preparing to slip away into the shadows when a soft, searching voice reached him. The words were not harsh or unruly as he had heard they would be, and the revelation of it all was that he understood them.

Ray pushed his eyes from behind his cover, taking a clear view of the other. Her face flushed with fright yet a genuine sense of gratitude fixed in her grimace.

"Thank you," intoned the soft voice again.

Ray poked his head out from the undergrowth, his eyes filled with intent. The face that greeted him was warm and inviting, not hostile like the others. He saw no ill will in the eyes, no hidden intent, only sincerity.

"Who are you?" the voice asked, apparently unafraid.

Ray shrank back down, yelling in a half-hearted tone, "Go

away! Take your wet and go away!"

"Go away? That's rather an odd thing for someone who just saved my life to say. Wouldn't you agree?"

Ray listened to the voice, adhering to the words, still shocked he could understand them with little difficulty. She spoke with an odd twang to her words, but the voice was soft. He didn't move or offer anything further. In his mind's eye, he saw the others he had seen before. He saw them stalk to the edge of his home and tear it up. "Go away!" he threw out again.

He heard a low rattle and a grumble as the other did precisely what he had asked.

He shot a hesitant glance towards the retreating form. "Wait!" he commanded. The girl stopped, turning back expectantly. Ray stood, immediately shrank back down. "What is your name?" he asked, not knowing what else to say.

***

"My name? What is your name?"

"Why would you want to know my name?"

Kerry shot back, "For the same reason you want to know mine."

Ray said nothing.

"You saved my life. I owe you a debt."

"You owe me nothing."

"Untrue, and if you're not going to say anything else,

good-bye…" Kerry was playing with him now, trying to coax him from hiding. She knew how to play this game well; this was how she had earned Waring's affections.

As she hurried away, playing with him, she was also curious. She had glimpsed the other for only a moment, but what she had saw in that moment stunned and attracted her as the lure attracted her Waring.

"Nothing out there. It is all waste," Stirling had told her of the place where they gathered the life liquid. "Its only purpose is for us to apply to the trees so that they may bear meat and to drink when we thirst. You stay away unless you have needs. Strange beasts lie there. Men have ventured out never to return, swallowed whole by the beasts of the wild."

She knew the faces of those beasts very well from her earliest childhood recollection to her most recent nightmare. The great crockin abounded in the lore and in life. She had seen their strange heads adorning testaments to the wild beyond preserved in the special houses. It was said the wizard got power from them.

She felt a chill in the air as the wind stirred, blowing hollowly down the face of the slant. Her pace quickened, though she only took a few more steps before she turned to stare back. "Where are you, Waring?" she asked of the wind, stopping just short of casting a shrill whistle after the gale that was gradually wafting along the hill.

She wouldn't be so afraid if she knew the other was near. She replayed the face she had seen in her mind. The dark, fierce countenance, the short thin body, barely clothed. She saw him lunge at her and grab her, and she started to run away, suddenly realizing what she saw was an image in her mind.

"Are you still there?" she called out, not understanding the curiosity attached to her attraction.

***

Ray stepped out from behind the camouflage, shouldering his pack, raising his arm in a sign of hailing. "I am," he called back, not knowing the pull of the lure was equally set into him.

He saw the full, round face tucked into a partial smile, accentuated by thick lines—the laughing lines. The eyes beckoned him to come closer, and he did, again not knowing why. He shifted the weight of the pack until it was comfortably settled and then slowly crossed the length that separated them.

In his mind, he saw pale, white faces surrounding him and staring down at him, imagining himself slumped to the ground under their gawking gaze, a relentless circle of ominous gloom. He stopped, as he was about to touch the dry and the Out. He glanced up at her, down, looking back up with intrigue at the dangling gnarl of long, flowing hair, hair so light that it seemed to match the hue of the sun itself.

Scratching at his head, Ray pulled out a tangled, stubby, dark curl, catching sight of his hands as he did this, suddenly comparing his hands to hers. In the back of his mind he saw the other outsiders again, the men dressed in thick clothes with angry faces, crashing headlong into his world. He pulled back, turned away. The smoot had said Ray would make a choice this day and while Ray considered it yet ahead, he did not know that it had already passed the instant he had taken his first step in the other's defense.

"What is your name?" Kerry asked, moving back down the hill. "You haven't told me though I have already given you mine."

She regarded him from head to toe, wondering about the long, slender stick in his hand, the store on the back, and all sorts of other things. *Where had he come from?* She wondered. *And why was he here? And why wasn't she afraid?*

As the distance between them diminished, so did her apprehension and her first impression of him changed as well. Up close, he didn't look so scant and thin. Well, thin to be sure, though he was, perhaps, her equal in height. She couldn't be sure because the slant of the hill obscured the proportions somewhat.

Ray responded after long duress, "Ray, my name is Ray." He moved closer feeling the tough, gritty touch of the stone land upon his feet. He was unafraid now, his determination was wrought. "Why do you theft that which is not your own?" he asked.

"Theft?"

Ray coldly intoned, "Steal."

"Steal? I do not take anything that is not freely granted," Kerry hesitated, pointing a long finger, "If this is what you are implying that I steal."

"I am," said Ray, unaware that he stood firmly upon the dead land and the feeling of it wasn't as foreign as he had once thought.

Kerry puffed up her cheeks, walking away without saying anything further.

Ray followed her up to the flat of the hill, struggling to catch up to her fleeted, long legs. He went no further, however, his heart stopping as he glanced over his shoulder, down, down to the wet.

Kerry maneuvered around a falling off, coming to a rest on the far side of it opposite Ray, a seemingly safe distance. She could stop now and regard him with full intent.

Kerry coaxed up the courage to ask him another question, but not before she made a vibrant summons, the high-pitched tone causing him to wince. "What were you doing out there? And where is it that you come from? I have never seen the likes of you, and I have been all the way to Adalayia."

Kerry spoke with pride, disappointed with Ray's confused stare, which had not been the response she expected. She continued, "More than once, mind you. And I have gone it alone, having just returned no more than a few days ago. I have seen the wizard who rules the land."

Bewildered, Ray said nothing. He was uneasy with the distance that separated them as much as by her words, and so, as he would cross from house to house without much thought, he crossed the falling off in one all-ensuing leap. He registered the surprise on Kerry's face, matching it with his own smile. He himself was astonished at the ease with which he had made the swoop, although the landing had been rough. The land did not give beneath his feet, and so he had overcompensated.

Still, he was surprised—he had crossed the distance with ease. He dropped his pack and his staff, and readied to make another jump. He wanted to try again.

Kerry's face was drawn, her eyes wide. She touched a firm hand to his shoulder. Her voice was stern as she began, "No, don't. You must never do that again. The falling off has no bottom. Are you not afraid of the abyss?"

"Did I do something wrong? I don't understand."

"You crossed the..." Kerry's voice grew weak, "...falling off, you are unwary and unwelcome."

Ray bundled his face up with confusion, "I don't understand."

"Ha!" she said throwing up her hands, "You are as barbaric as—" She cut short her words, corrected herself. "You truly do not know?"

"Know what?" Ray asked.

"The falling off… Are you not afraid? Or do you not know fear?"

"Fear?"

"The falling off is endless. If you slip into it, you will never return. Do you understand? There is only one place where it can be crossed, and that is the bridge between City and Country. One place, remember that!"

Ray answered honestly, "I will," though he still wasn't sure exactly why.

The next question the two began at the same time, it was back to the why's and the how's, and the how come's. Slowly as they went back and forth, an odd sort of understanding grew out of their mutual curiosity. For each similarity they found, they discovered disparity and contradictions. They were different peoples and yet the same—and unwittingly, Ray drifted along behind the path his druthers had carved out for him.

The gray-faced land, the outer fringe of the land beyond the hill, the land of mourning, the still, dead land that Ray had dreaded for all his life, stretched out endlessly before him. He was so caught up in his conversation with Kerry that he didn't realize the enormity of it all. The simple fact was that he had made a conscious decision to help Kerry and that decision was changing and shaping his life.

Though countless deeds separated him from the path's end and innumerable twists and turns lay ahead, he was now a step further along the way. What this meant, he wouldn't know for some time, but he would later come to realize the point at which it all changed and the point at which he had put his feet upon the true path of his life. For now, he sighed, cast back his shoulders and followed the outsider girl. She for her part smiled, imagining the lure in his mouth, as if he were her Waring.

Chapter Ten:
Curiosity

Ray sat in Kerry's rocking chair, looking through the window, watching Kerry attend to the needs of a distant cousin of his familiar arbor. As he rocked back and forth, ignoring the dizzying sensation this gave him, he sometimes looked about the house, Kerry's word, not his own. Frustration, an aftereffect from conversing with Kerry, was still evident in his expression, not that he disliked Kerry. It was quite the contrary.

The two had quickly found that beyond basic speech, the

words they used, though often the same, held disparate meanings. Ray even found attempting to clarify his definition of something more difficult than if he had just ignored the questioning glances and plodded through what he had been attempting to say. Even in his sleep, he could sometimes hear the new words repeating over and over in his mind.

Kerry just thought Ray was thick-headed and their strange attraction grew regardless of these differences. She tended to her trees more often than she normally did, and in this way, she gave him time to wrestle with his own thoughts, thoughts which she knew were troubling him very deeply, thoughts that when he put them into words sometimes frightened her. He told her of things that though he had never seen he knew, and she knew they were true and real.

What was even more frightening was that he could describe in vivid detail Adalayia and places beyond that she had never seen but had heard about. He also told her of places she had never heard about: a stronghold perched atop Mount Lar, a stone canyon where dragon lizards roamed, a far away land called Korran where undermountain men dwelled, and a land beyond where all were equal and free. This place Ray called Frething. He claimed it was beautiful beyond compare and that the hand of the wizard did not extend there.

While she listened and was convinced he told the truth, she was also worried about Waring's disappearance. The collections had stopped altogether. She feared he was lost and would never return.

Doubts about Ray filled her mind as well. She wondered if the things he had told her about could be real. If there really were such places in the world. But then again, all her ideals about the world were in doubt. Up until a few days ago, her thoughts went no further than City and Country, but now such innocent thoughts were in jeopardy. Ray had showed her, if only by his appearance, that she truly knew little about the world around her.

She was curious. No, more than curious. Could a place of such as Frething exist, and if it did indeed exist, and Ray could find it, what then? Did she really want to leave her home, the place she had known all her life, the place Stirling had bade her to stay in and she had promised that she would. But Stirling had been wrong before. He had been wrong about the wizard and the tax. Not paying the tax had cost him his life, and Kerry now had to work to repay his debt and her own.

The very thought of debt and work, brought her to the present, and the task before her. Two mouths to feed meant more work for her in gathering the offerings. Ray had taken a liking to the meat of the tree, surprised that each conveyed variety in taste and texture depending on the tree and her desires. She had tried the light and the dark, as Ray called it, and disliked it. She thought of these things foul-tasting roots, though she never told Ray this. The bittersweet, on the other hand, appealed to the tiny twinge of craving she sometimes had, and so she favored it over all the other things Ray had introduced her to.

Humming a wordless tune, Kerry labored around the trees, setting them into frenzied vibrations as she finally applied the life liquid, the wet as Ray named it, for the third and final time this day. A passing glance toward the house revealed Ray's weighted gaze was still upon her, and she recalled another thing that she had been mulling over previously. A thing she did not know how she would explain to Ray or how he would take it when she did.

The problem she had was with True. The small beast gave her chill dreams at night. She pictured it wrapped around her throat, twisting, and her gasping, gasping for air she couldn't quite grasp. The thought of it even now gave her cold shivers.

Turning back, she cast Ray a glum smile. She wanted to like True, mind you, and she told herself this, but her subconscious had conflicting notions.

Soon afterward she finished her chores and returned indoors, vaguely aware that as she did this, Ray was no longer seated by the window. She turned a full circle, finding the room empty, hearing muffled laughter. "Ray, where are you?"

No reply came.

"Ray?"

A subtle chuckle.

Kerry turned about again. "Ray," she said, her tone slightly miffed.

"Outside," said Ray, having slipped out the door.

"The sun will set soon," she admonished.

Ray stepped back inside, "I know. Come on, hurry up."

"Hurry up for what?" asked Kerry. "We shouldn't be outside now. The soldiers may come, and I'm not ready yet."

Ray ignored her words. "I'll show you if you hurry. We can be there and back before sunset."

"Where and back before sunset? We could get lost in the dark. I don't like the night, Ray, you know that."

"Don't worry. I have very good eyes," Ray coaxed away her objection, pulling her after him. "Can't you smell it?" he asked.

"Smell what?" Kerry didn't smell anything.

"Take a deep breath, feel the sense of vibrancy in the air. Can you not smell it?" Ray was excited now, running away from her, beckoning her to chase him. Kerry followed. Ray led her along the twisted trail that he now knew fairly well.

By now, they had come quite some distance and she was regarding the dark sky in front of them. "Why are we going this way? It will be dark soon. Ray, it is a dark omen and it will bring ill tidings. We must not go this way."

She stopped, grabbed his hands to force him to look at her.

"Ray, if the soldiers ever come, you must not be seen. Do not be alarmed by their actions. In the Country, we do as we must. You must let me deal with them. Do you understand?"

"Have you thought about what I've said? It is past time for me to be off. I must journey to the stone land to follow my path. Will you go with me as we've discussed?"

Kerry's serious expression didn't waver. "Ray, I can never leave. My home is Country, I am Country. I have made a promise. .... It's time to return to the house. It's safest there."

Ray ran off, stopped, circled back and dragged her along behind him. "Nonsense, you said you never saw it rain. Can't you smell it? Isn't this wonderful?" To be truthful Ray always thought of rain as an irritation, but Kerry didn't know that. Ray didn't stop at the edge of the In. He meant to drag her along after him.

Her shriek brought him to in immediate stop. Panic and fright lit Kerry's face. "Stop, no! What are you doing? I don't want to! Ray, let go of me! I don't want to see it! I'm going home now!" And with that, she retreated.

Ray already had his feet in the wet and it felt so good that he was hard pressed to turn away. Perhaps he should have immediately pursued her, though he didn't, and when at last he did pursue her, she was already gone from sight. It was strikingly odd how the simple touch of the wet drove back familiar thoughts about the gray land he traveled over—

thoughts he had considered behind him.

When he returned, Kerry was rapidly swaying back and forth in the old rocker, soothing away harsh thought. She said nothing as he closed the door. The sun had set as she said it would. The omen she had perceived was commanded forward and Kerry fought hard to drive it away, repeating soft words in her mind, words her mother had taught to her, words that would chase away the evil.

Ray stumbled through the apology, an apology that was left hanging in the air about them for some time. "I'm sorry, I just thought… Well… You know what I was trying to… I'm sorry, O.K."

Ray tended to True, cleaning his friend's coat until it shone finely. True was growing sleek and long, and there was a continual bulge in his midsection as Ray saw to it that his small companion was fed well. There were rodents about, and other small hapless creatures that True fancied.

The last of the great orange bubble had disappeared, or at least that is how Kerry thought of the sunset this night when she finally broke away from the window. "Tell me more of your dreams?" she asked, "Are there really such places? Tell me of the bridge… I mean, crossing," she said using his word.

Ray didn't look up. "I don't know if I can. I don't think I was supposed to tell you in the first place."

"You're not supposed to tell me? What is that supposed to

mean?"

Ray slumped back onto the bed. He was more tired than usual. "This friend of yours you spoke of, when is he going to return?"

Kerry laughed, "I don't think very soon."

"What do you mean by that? Why are you laughing? Did I say something funny?"

Kerry spied the glare in his eye, "Silly, Waring is not a man. He is a beast," she stopped, corrected, "Well he is a friend of mine, that part is true." She hesitated again. "I led you to believe he was a man so you wouldn't think I was alone here. Waring is a beast of flight."

"A buzzer?" asked Ray. He could only imagine an insect.

"No," shot back Kerry with a frown, "a beast with wings." She gestured with her hands to give him an indication of size.

Ray's eyes grew wide, his face flushed. He didn't understand how a winged beast could be nearly as big as a man. "Are you playing with me again?"

"Well maybe a little, he's not that big actually. More like this." Kerry raised one hand above the other, showing that Waring was as tall as her forearm, and then she gestured with her hands to show Waring's impressive wingspan again.

The wingspan was what confused Ray. He had never seen a bird with such a wingspan. "And he flies?" Ray registered the look in her eyes. "Where is this flying beast then?"

Kerry searched for a more suitable word, a word that had a clearer meaning to her, though it was not a word she would use to describe her Waring. "He is a falkish," she said thinking it would enlighten Ray, not realizing until too late that it just confused the matter. Hastily, she cut him off, saying, "Tell me of the colored bans in the sky again."

"Rain wash," tossed back Ray, throwing the word out as an insult, just as she had done to him—the way he saw it.

A lull fell on them once more. Ray allowed his eyes to slip closed as he listened to the swaying of the rocker, allowing it to ease away his tensions just as if he were seated upon it, just as he knew Kerry used it to cure her own woes.

"I only dreamt of it that once, but it was like nothing I ever saw. Ephramme's father said he saw one once, said it was just floating in the sky like nothing he ever saw before, golden, red and blue. I suppose he's the one that brought on my dream, but I could see it on the sky so clearly. It was almost as if I could just reach out and lay a hand on it," Ray said as if Kerry was in Third Village that day, going on and on and on.

"…and then I woke up," he said, returning her from the dream. What he neglected to tell her though was that was the day Waddymarre returned from his journey, and that was the day of his second-father's passing, all before Ray was even born. "…and then I awoke," Ray said again.

Chapter Eleven:
The Stone Land

"Ray, wake up, wake up! Hurry, please!" Kerry intoned, bending low, screaming into his ear, her voice stricken with anxiety. "Hurry, Ray, hurry! You have to go!"

Ray stirred, sleep still embroidered onto his eyes. "What? Is something wrong?"

Kerry ran to the window, mumbling to herself, "Oh, it's too late, quickly, under the bed. Go, go!" She gave him a tempered glare, reinforcing her words. "Go, Ray, and remember, no matter what happens—" Kerry moved to the door, checking the bolts. "—No matter what happens, you must not move! Promise me this, Ray... Promise?"

"Okay, I promise," Ray said, still rather sleepy. It was early. There was scant light in the room. He eased under the bed.

Feverishly, Kerry straightened out the edge of the sheets as she surveyed the chamber and tossed Ray's pack into a corner, concealing it as best she could. She slipped True's cage down to Ray, whispering after it, "Remember your promise." Ray grumbled that he would.

It was then that a heavy pounding stifled a breath in Kerry's throat. The door shook violently under the weighted blows.

"Y-e-e-sss?" answered Kerry, feigning a yawn. "Who is it?"

A stoic voice returned, so powerful in fact that even if Kerry had covered her ears with both hands and thrust her head under the nearby pillow she would have heard it. "You are mandated to open this door in the name of the Great High Wizard of Adalayia!"

Kerry didn't move. The pounding did not stop. "Yes, what is it?" she calmly asked despite the order.

Faces pressed into the windows just then, and Kerry knew enough to move to the door. The summons was repeated. "You are mandated to open this door in the name of the Great High Wizard of Adalayia!"

"Just a moment," flashed Kerry, seemingly angry at the

disturbance. "What is it that you seek?"

The blows at the door increased. "You have until the time I finish my words to open this door or we will bash it down. What is your response?"

Kerry swung the door open not a moment to soon, the ram swished through the air in front of her, pulled back by strong hands. "Yes?" she asked, brushing pretended petals of sleep from her eyes.

With the door unsealed, the others did not stop. Kerry could only watch and count them as they stormed into her house. They took table, chairs and her favored rocker, flinging them against the walls and out the windows, dashing them into a thousand tiny splinters. Kerry ran to the bed and plopped down on top of it. "No please, take no more, I beg of you!"

"This is the punishment for refusing my call," warned the stern-voiced man.

"I was asleep," cried Kerry, hurrying tears to her eyes, both real and feigned. The rocker had held a dear place in her heart and now it lay splintered, half of it splashed beneath the window and the other half teetering upon the window's broken frame.

The other did not turn his cold, probing eyes away from her. "When we return tomorrow, see that you act accordingly."

"Return? What do you mean return? I have nothing, there is nothing I can give you. You are weeks ahead of schedule," screamed Kerry.

"Watch your tongue or I will have it removed," the man spoke with venom and in such a way that Kerry wholly believed he would, "You gave no tithe and so this is your punishment. You are warned. We will return tomorrow."

"The promised delivery was for three weeks hence, I've only just returned from Adalayia. His lordship vowed by City and Country the debt would be put aside until then." Kerry gulped for air, cooling her temper, "I truly have nothing to offer you. I did not know I was to give tithe until three weeks hence."

"Is this your scrawl upon the book of markets?" he demanded as another at his side produced a large tome.

"I'm not sure," stated Kerry, taking a step forward, "maybe it is…"

"Either it is or it isn't. There are no maybes…" Anger flowed to the man's gruff face.

Kerry took a closer look, "Yes," she said, lying. She couldn't be sure. She couldn't read—reading wasn't a skill Stirling had taught her. She had only made a mark as Stirling had showed her. Suddenly, she recalled something she had forgotten, something that she only now understood. Stirling was a proud man, and even while her mother had been there, he had told them both to wait while he went into the market house. Now she understood the purpose of the quarter stack that was laid carefully aside come winter collection time. The quarter stack her father carried into the market house that was never seen again.

"When we return, we will take three times our normal share," and then he tossed in, "Good day…" as he beckoned his men to withdraw.

"I cannot get that much meat in one day. The trees do not produce that much so fast. You have to give me more time," argued Kerry, feeling a sudden surge of bravado as they swept from her home.

"Fine, fine," chuckled the man, "you shall have all the time you will require…" He stopped, his grimace broadening as he watched a look of gratitude grow on Kerry's face. "One day, no more no less, and if you do not produce the tithe, perhaps we will take something else next time… Something more precious that you can ever imagine."

Kerry shuddered. "But I can't…"

The man adeptly cut her off as he took a step toward her and reached a gloved hand out to her face, grabbing hold of the underside of her chin. His hand was large and powerful and his fingers stemmed from ear to ear. He twisted her face up as if in a vise. "You will," he intoned, his face pulled so close to hers that Kerry felt his stank breath on her skin and smelled it as she inhaled painfully.

With his other hand, he slapped her face. "Don't ever speak back to me again. You will do what I command."

Kerry heard a faint scratching from behind her. Hastily, she slumped back onto the bed, concealing the low moan, with a mighty sob, "I will, I will do it. Please leave now, please."

The other seemed to like the desperate look on her face and it made him smile wryly again. "It is good that we understand each other. You know, City would probably suit you best. This is no place to be alone."

"I'm…" Kerry yanked to a halt. "I'm thinking about it."

The man smiled in approval, exiting without further delay. Kerry watched him go, real, thick, vibrant tears issuing forth the instant the door clicked closed. She curled up onto the bed, shivering uncontrollably, fighting to pull herself together.

Ray could cower no longer. He sprang out from under the bed, wielding his fists into the air wildly. He had not heard the other leave and he was indeed surprised when he found the other had gone.

"Kerry, are you alright? Did he hurt you? So help me if he did—"

"No, he didn't. Get back! They may return. You mustn't be found," her words were sincere.

"I am going nowhere!" persisted Ray.

Kerry put a hand to his shoulder. "There is nothing you can

do. This is my own problem, and I will deal with it." With a final shudder, she seized up the tears in her eyes, and collected herself, touching a cloth to her face, and pushing back her hair. She stood and walked to the door then. "Stay here," she commanded, "I will return soon."

Ray ran to the door and cut off her exodus. "Where are you going? You're not going anywhere without me," he objected.

"I must talk to the trees and gather the wet..." she stopped and corrected herself, "the life liquid... You must remain here." The mistake showed just how much of an influence Ray had on her life at the moment. If he had stopped to put his arms around her and to tell her everything would be all right, perhaps she would have stayed and listened to his words, but he did not. Instead, he backed away from the door.

"I will go with you," insisted Ray.

Kerry's strong-minded spirit took over, "No, you will remain here! If they see you, there is no telling what they will do to you. You must stay inside and out of sight. It is for your own protection."

Although Ray said nothing more, he appealed to her with his eyes. "Let me go with you," the expression read, "I will be alright. We will be alright." Kerry had a differing opinion; she closed the door behind her as she departed.

Ray began clearing the mess within the house. His heart

was shattered, similar to the broken rocker. While he picked up the pieces and straightened out the mess, there wasn't much else he could do. He did not know the art of the builder, and so all he could do was look at the pile of shattered dreams, wishing they would become chairs, table and rocker again.

Meanwhile outside, Kerry greeted the fallow sun, which seemed so remote and indifferent to her plight. She whispered words of the winter harvest to the trees, chasing after them words of her own. "I know, I know," she said, "you have just given, but you must give again. There is need, great need. Will you do this for me?" She asked permission, even though she knew they would do as she bade regardless. "Will you do this for me?" she repeated.

Kerry hummed to calm her nerves, telling herself that it eased the frets of the trees as well. She applied the life liquid, a full day's supply in one dosage, and then she was off to make the long trek to the edge of the world. The edge of the wet, she corrected herself.

As she hurried on her way, Ray slunk out of the house, crouching low, sometimes walking on hands and knees to stay abreast with her. There was no way he was going to let her go alone and his thin form slipped in nicely amongst the shadows.

Ray stayed at the top of the hill. He did not venture into the open, though he remained alert watching for the smallest hint of movement from either the wet or the dry. Morning was a favored feeding time for slither and bull, but Ray did not scrutinize for them alone, he also kept a close eye on the edge of the Out, knowing those men could return at any time. As Kerry started up the hill, Ray pulled back, remaining out of sight.

Kerry sang to the trees again, and this was the very first time Ray ever discerned the words. The song was beautiful. Ray had never heard a voice carried thus, so pristine it seemed. He could almost envision the words floating on the air, each radiating out to one by one, setting leaves to quivering and the trees' bowels to action.

Ray was sad when the song ended, its conclusion so unexpected that he almost tumbled from the shadows. He had been leaning his chin against his hand, head down and heavy, and while he had not noticed it then he had been swaying to the song.

Ray followed Kerry to the edge of the wet three more times that day, wondering at her strength of conviction. He also listened to her song three more times that day and by the time the last word drifted across to the trees, the words and the song were etched indelibly into his mind where they repeated ceaselessly. Kerry truly had a gift and Ray was in awe of it.

Ray watched her stroke the trees now, coaxing them with kind words, words that Ray could no longer understand.

Taking advantage of opportune timing, Ray slowly graduated towards the house, slipping indoors without making a sound. He crawled past the window, eased onto the bed. He pulled the covers up around him, sealing his eyes and feigning deep sleep.

Indeed Ray was asleep when Kerry came into the abode. The day had been draining and he was in the midst of a dream as her footsteps awoke him. Her eyes were downtrodden as she turned to greet him. He rubbed true sleep from his eyes. "Sunset so soon?" he asked.

Kerry nurtured the surprise from her eyes. Asleep! She was outraged for an instant. She had fancied him her champion and instead, he slept. "Yes," she responded glumly.

"What do you think they will do when they return tomorrow? Will they take the…" Ray searched for the proper word, "fruit and leave? Or do you think they really want something else?"

Ray's words only reinforced Kerry's worries. She hoped they would leave if she provided what they asked for. "I think so," she said as if offering to the very air around her to make the choice.

Ray sat straight up, moved to the end of the bed, his eyes wide. "What if we left before they arrived? What then? We could go. In hours we could be far away from here and you would not have to worry about anything." Ray stopped, his head sagged heavily as his words seemed to be lost on her, wasted.

Ray began again, his voice containing a rare quality, the portent of known truth. "There is nothing here for you, Kerry. You told me this yourself. What I saw is real; it is out there. We have only to believe and we will find it. I saw the truth of it upon the old smoot's face and in his eyes, in Waddymarre's eyes, my father's eyes. I will reach the place he could never find. I will find the place of dreams and make it real. He knew this when he sent me out and he all but told me so with his eyes, powerful probing eyes."

Ray believed and that simple truth was enough to make his views not only reach out to Kerry, but to shake her soul violently and rend apart simple thought. However, one thing held her back. "Ray," Kerry drank in Ray's deep stare, "I cannot leave. I made a promise. I must stay…"

"If you made a previous promise to stay, make me a new promise that you will go. And then we will go together, you and I! It's not safe for you here, you must know that."

"Ray, I cannot. I must stay here. I must tend to Waring. He will return and if I am not here… If I am not here, who knows what will happen to him."

Ray threw a plea into the air, much like Kerry's own, though he wished for a different thing that he hoped would come true. He would have to wait and see, but he hoped it wouldn't be too much longer. The stone land was calling to him, and in his dreams the wizard seemed somehow closer than he'd ever been before.

Chapter Twelve:
Discovery and Escape

Kerry awoke first, before the sun even considered appearing in the distant east. She was gripped with stark, real fear and a mundane, unhappy task lay before her.

During the long night, she hadn't slept much. The floor was hard and ungiving. Ray had offered her the bed, but she had refused. The rocker—which was now broken—was the only place she could find sleep anyway and one of them needed to have coherent thoughts come morning.

Ray would wake soon. She knew this and so she hurried.

In the dark, she followed the long path from her home, raising the call to all listening ears, though her Waring was not to be found.

Sorrowfully, with the arrival of dawn she returned, her one chance banished. The meat was plentiful though. The trees had produced as she had asked, for which she thanked them.

She began to gather the meat and soon had enough to last the two of them many days. She would be sad when she had to give it away to those who wouldn't appreciate it.

Ray's pack lay in the middle of the floor, appearing more full than usual. Kerry took note of the blankets and bedroll perched on top of it. Two canisters sat beside it, canisters that she knew had been empty the day before and were now filled. Ray was hunched over tidying seals, almost ready to lift the pack to his shoulders as he heard her enter.

"We are going. Your things are stowed," was all he said. Ray shouldered the pack, adjusting under the heavy weight awkwardly until it was settled.

"But Waring," lamented Kerry, "I cannot leave him."

Ray looked her in the eye. "Apparently, he is well enough to fend for himself."

"You don't understand. If he returns and I am not here, he will never come back and I will lose him." Unhappily, Kerry gazed around the room. "If we go, where will we go to?"

His retort was simple, "To Adalayia."

Kerry stopped him from passing through the door. "No, Ray. You can't go to Adalayia. You don't understand what will happen to you if you go there. The people there will not understand you or your kind. You will not like it."

They set to arguing. Her inventing reasons why she must stay and him countering with reasons she must go with him. To him leaving was a thing that must be done, and her going with him was also a thing that must be done. He decided right then though that he would tell her nothing of his latest dream—the dream which she was a part of, the dream in which she rode upon the back of a dragon lizard and the skies were full of great flying beasts.

A scratching at the door startled them both. Instant silence followed. Ray quickly reverted to the ways of the In, seeking both to defend himself and to get distance between himself and the thing that had startled him. He was scarcely more than a few steps away before he returned to Kerry's side however. She for her part, didn't move. Ray thought her bold but perhaps foolish. Anyone who was foolish enough to stay in the path of a bull was swept away and pulled down to the depths.

A shrill call sounded, followed by a rough tapping. Ray was certain the soldiers had returned and it was now too late to run. What would they do? How would they defend themselves? Could they defend themselves? They had no weapons, no protective clothing.

Both were spellbound, frozen in place, waiting for impending doom. The window, thought Ray, they would slip out the window. The scratching returned, there was the call again.

A curious grin crossed Kerry's face. A fire returned to her downtrodden eyes. Ray was trying to move her to the window but she refused. She moved instead to the door and when she swung the door open, he mistook her startled gasp of wonder as horror.

He dropped the heavy pack to the floor with a thud, and whirled around, staff in hand, ready to strike. A strike he nearly followed through with when confronted by the wary beast. The falkish had returned, almost as if on cue. Kerry's calls and Ray's prayers had not gone unanswered.

The falkish seemed to take an instant liking to Ray, as he did to it. Ray had never seen such a beast, clad in gray, black and brown feathers. Waring did not remain still for long, quickly returning to his high-pitched calls, then just as suddenly settling onto the crossed stave planted before the door. As Waring swept across the room Ray got full view of the immense wingspan for the first time and was undeniably awed.

"Where were you, you naughty boy?" asked Kerry, stroking the falkish's head. "Go on, tell me?" she repeated, "No need to be shy with company and all."

Kerry soothed Waring's ruffled feathers. "Is that so," she responded. "Well you'll just have to tell her, you are mine and I will not let go of you ever again."

Ray was hesitant to interfere, doing so only after allowing a short period of silence to follow. "You can speak to it?" he asked amazed.

"Of course, silly," Kerry said.

Ray thought it unnecessary to remark on this. "We had better be off. There is no telling when they will come. Do you know which way they will come from?"

"Don't you think we ought to think this through? This is so sudden. I'm not so sure I want to go anywhere, Ray."

Kerry struggled with inner demons. In her mind's eye she saw Stirling urging her to stay. The Country was her home; the City was no place for her and it certainly wasn't a place for Ray. As Kerry spoke, she seemed to be considering her own words. "If I go, there can be no turning back. No turning back and I will lose the only home I've ever known."

She started to tremble and a quiver set to her cheek as she heard voices far off, echoing down from high up in the hills.

"Home is where and what we make it, Kerry," Ray told her, "I know this as I know no other thing. The land beyond is there, I know it. My father saw it in his dreams and so have I—and I cannot rest until I try." He hesitated for a moment, then he told her of his latest dream, the dream of which she was a part. "You mustn't be afraid to try, Kerry. ... We must go no before it is too late."

In her mind's eye, she saw it then: the land beyond the beyond. She saw the rain wash and the great washfalls that Ray had told her about. And then strangely, she saw Stirling standing tall, holding her mother's hand, pride showing in his eyes. The sense of pride was fleeting though as his eyes and face betrayed concern, anguish.

Her vision then became the embodiment of her fears and the very reality of the voices in the distance fell upon her. "Do we make a pact?"

Ray asked, "A pact?"

"An agreement to stand by our word: no turning back, Ray. Once we start there can be no turning back. If you can't agree to this, I can't go. I would sooner remain here. You always have a home to return to. For me, if I leave there will be none, only that which I make for myself." Kerry spit into her hand and held it out to Ray. "Do you understand?"

Ray spit into his hand, touched it to hers. "Yes, I understand."

"There are few trails from this side to Adalayia and none past it as you wish to go. We must go through the city. There is no other way. Are you prepared for that? Do you understand what might happen?" Kerry was being rational.

"Don't worry, I will find a way through the city. We will

find a way, together." He believed his words, for he had seen them both in places far off and away from Adalayia. He added, "Don't forget where it is that I come from——"

"How could I?" cut in Kerry, "How will you get through? They will see you?"

"We will worry about that then and not now," offered Ray, eager to be off.

Kerry read his agitation. "They returned to that trail yesterday. We must take this one." She pointed off to the right. "It is the longest and hardest way to through the stone land and to the city. It wraps and winds its way through many twisted trails. I have never been that way, Ray."

True, who had wrestled his way free from the cage, came to a rest beneath Ray's feet. The slither's eyes were fixed on the falkish; its tongue flashing in and out. "We must leave now. Hurry!"

"Did he talk to you?" Kerry asked, intrigued.

"No," whined Ray, yet as he thought about it, he wasn't sure. *Why had an alarm sounded in his mind?* Regardless, True knew enough to return to the confines of the cage and Ray knew enough not to trouble himself needlessly.

It was then that they heard voices from below the hill and not just those from the men coming down the long trail above.

Kerry had her own pack, the front shoulder pack she used

to carry the meat to winter market. Nothing would be left for the soldiers to carry away. Kerry sang a soothing, sad song to her trees, a solemn song of parting and remembrance. Someday I will return, she promised them in her song, though she did not tell Ray this.

A quake shifted through the trees and Ray swore he saw the great boughs of the trees bend and shift, waving a goodbye as he and Kerry departed.

The words of the song were again lost to Ray, though he did not need to comprehend the words to understand their beauty. The song was captivating and Kerry sang it long after they had departed, taking to humming it much later.

A land rougher and tougher than Ray had ever fathomed spread out before them. The path they followed was narrow and old, yet Ray was unafraid as he took Kerry's hand and they walked hand in hand, deeper and deeper into the stone land.

This was the path his dreams had spoken of and though he had not seen the outsider girl in his earliest dreams, she was part of his dreams now. He was optimistic that together they would reach the land beyond and that he return one day to tell Tall, Keen, Isaac, Ephramme and the others about his journey. He was confident too that when he did, Kerry would be beside him.

With the voices chasing behind them in the distance, Ray and Kerry hurried away, hoping against hope to escape safely into the wilds, to make passage to Adalayia, through Adalayia, and eventually beyond. There could be no turning back now and they both knew it. Their fear of the unknown was their shield, making them more aware of their surroundings, and perhaps, even giving them awareness of their greatest hope of all—that such a far off place existed and that they could reach it.

End of Book One
The Story continues with:

Magic Lands: Into the Stone Land

BONUS EXCERPT
FROM

KEEPER MARTIN'S TALES

BY

ROBERT STANEK

KEEPER
MARTIN'S TALES

Crying out into the darkness, alone, afraid and drenched in sweat, Vilmos awoke. His thoughts raced. The whole of his small body shivered uncontrollably. Opening eyes and uncurling his huddled form from a corner, moist with his own perspiration yet still cold from the night's chill, was a slow, time-consuming process.

"It was only a nightmare," Vilmos whispered to reassure himself—a nightmare like no other. In the dream he had used the forbidden magic once too often and the Priests of the Dark Flame—opposers of all that is magic and magical—came from their temples to slay him.

Vilmos stood uneasily and dipped trembling hands into the washbasin beside the bed. The cool water sucked the hurt from his eyes and mind and gently began to soothe and awaken his senses as nothing else could.

Carefully he dabbed a wet cloth to the corners of his eyes and only then did he become something other than the frightened boy who in his dreams huddled into the forlorn corner because of the sense of security it gave him to know his back was against the wall and that nothing could sneak up on him from behind.

Only then that he became the boy of twelve whose name was Vilmos. Vilmos because it was a trustworthy name. Vilmos because it was his father's name, who was named Vilmos because it had been his father's name. Vilmos, the Counselor's son.

Readying for the day's chores, Vilmos pushed the last of the dream from his thoughts. He dressed quickly and slipped on his ill-fitting boots as he stumbled toward the kitchen.

The aroma of fresh-baked black bread and honey cakes pungent in the air about the kitchen, mixing with the growling of his stomach, made him aware of an enormous hunger. The night had been unbearably long and he had not eaten since supper of the previous day.

"Late again. You'll sleep your life away. Already an hour past first light," said his mother. She stood in front of the hearth. The words were not meant to be harsh, nor were they taken thus. They were a standard greeting.

"I know mother, I am sorry," replied Vilmos, tossing gnarled hair to one side surreptitiously, hair that should have been combed. He started to hurry away.

"Vilmos, where are you going?" Lillath asked. "Must I always remind you of your lessons? Someday you will fill your father's position. Someday you will be Counselor of Tabborrath Village. Now, recite the lore of the peoples."

"Mother, do I have to?"

Lillath didn't say anything, she just stared.

"Can I use the book?"

"From memory."

"The tale of the Four Peoples is the lore of four kingdoms," Vilmos began, beaming with Lillath's smile upon him. "Small in number, strong of will, united they stood against powerful kingdoms of the North. Four vast kingdoms would conquer the Four Peoples, but the will of the Four Peoples was too strong. Lycya, mightiest of the kingdoms, was swallowed by barren desert. North Reach and the clans over-mountain were consumed by the twenty-year snow. Queen of Elves and all her people were washed into West Deep by the three-year rain. Only the Alder's kingdom, once the smallest kingdom of the North, survives.

"To survive, the Alder's kingdom formed an alliance with the Four Peoples. Their Graces, King Alexas of Yug, King Jarom of Vostok, King Peter of Zapad and his Royal Majesty,

King Charles of Sever, are the wardens of the Four Peoples. The four wardens maintain the alliance and protect the Four Peoples."

Lillath maintained her smile. "Well, yes," she said, "that is the lore of the four kingdoms and thus the tale of Four Peoples. But it is not *the* lore of the Four Peoples. You need to take great care in your listening. Listening is the counselor's greatest skill. Each tale, each bit of lore, tells a lesson. Relate the lesson through the lore; it is the way of the counselor. Choose the wrong tale, give the wrong advice. Do you understand?"

"Yes, mother."

"Now tell me the correct tale and guess the lesson."

Nervously, Vilmos played his tongue against his cheek. "From memory?"

"You may use the book if need be, at times even your father reads from the book."

"Mother," began Vilmos, looking into her eyes with much sincerity, "is it not time to—"

"Run along," she said. "Wood for the day's fire." There was a hint of mirth in her voice as she watched him wet his hands and settle his unruly hair.

Vilmos briefly, but closely, studied his mother's features as he did each morning. Offset by a touch of gray, dark black hair the color of a starless night sky fell to her waist. Her face, ripened with age in a pleasant way, was deep-set with eyes of hazel that seemed always to be calling out. This morning they said, *Hurry along or you'll be late.*

He looked like her, not like father, thought Vilmos each morning as he did this—a father who barely tolerated him. Harsh words chased through the boy's mind. "Vilmos, why did you do that? I told you not to!" or "Vilmos, go to your room." With an occasional, "I should send him away," thrown in when his father thought Vilmos couldn't hear.

"He is only a boy," Vilmos often heard in rebuke. "He will change in time. Give him more time." There was a deep love between the two, mother and son.

Wood for the hearth could be gathered easily from the brambles on the edge of the thick woods near the outskirts of the village and it was to this place that Vilmos started to go, but the outside air this morning was chillier than usual and it sent a shiver racing down Vilmos' back. It carried with it sadness and a sudden flood of remembrance. In the back of his mind, Vilmos knew the real reason he watched his mother so closely. One day he would indeed be sent away, far away, because one day the dark priests would come for him.

Vilmos returned to the house to collect his short cloak. As he ran through the kitchen he stopped beside his mother. Rising up on the tips of his toes, he gave her a single peck on her cheek. For an instant, a smile broke her tired face and fondly she touched hand to cheek.

"That's better," Vilmos shouted to no one in particular as he ran outside, slipping the sleeves of his shielding cloak into place. He could endure the cold now, and in a way, the memory as well.

"Hurry, breakfast!" shouted Lillath after him, while unconsciously raising a hand to her cheek once more where soft, young lips had touched. Vilmos looked back only for a moment to see this and to catch her eye. She added as he dashed away, "Remember to be careful… Remember what happened to the girl from Olex Village."

***

Out of breath from the long run, Vilmos doubled over. The sharp pain in his sides told him the run had been especially good. The way he figured it, if the walk from his father's house to the edge of the woods took thirty minutes one way and he ran it in five, he had nearly an hour to do whatever he pleased.

After the pain and the spots before his eyes passed, Vilmos quickly stretched. He knew from experience if his leg muscles were too tense or if he strained a muscle, he'd have to walk—or limp—home. Upon finishing, he put on his boots. He preferred to run barefoot; otherwise, the boots gave him blisters.

The air grew suddenly cold as an icy wind howled up the little country path that parted the dark wood. It was then that

Vilmos noticed how quiet the woods were that morning.

He stared long into the dark wood—keeper of his secrets—as he often did. Here his childhood dreams had been realized. In the shadow of the great trees, he could run screaming as loud as he pleased, slay fire-breathing dragons by the score, discover incredible lost treasures, play with imaginary friends, and still return home on time—well, usually.

Vilmos easily collected a large bundle of light wood from the nearby thicket, and then laid it aside. The wind howled. He stared up the overgrown path. He never ventured very far into the woods—only far enough to be within their shadows, yet close enough to still see the sunlight of the clearing beyond.

He heard what sounded like footsteps. He turned and stared, but saw only shadows. An alarm went off in his mind. He picked up a large branch and wielded it before him.

"Hello?" he called out, "Is someone there?"

Movement in the shadows caught his eye. For an instant, he could have sworn he saw an old man carrying a gnarled cane.

"Hel-lo?"

Holding the stick before him, in what to him seemed a menacing pose, Vilmos crept into the shadows of the dark woods. Leaves crunched beneath his boots. He grimaced.

Movement caught his careful eye again. He turned, raising the stick, ready to strike, then stopped cold. He saw a mound of black fur and dark eyes, a great black bear, kin of the much smaller browns the village huntsmen often sought.

The giant bear was no more than five feet away.

Two days ago in Olex Village, one of the three villages in their cluster, a young girl had been mauled to death by a bear. Vilmos didn't want to share her fate. He stood perfectly still, his heart racing so fast it seemed to want to jump out of his chest. Then the great beast reared up on its hind legs. Terror gripped Vilmos' mind. Warm urine raced down his legs. His every thought told him to run, but he couldn't. It was as if he was frozen to the spot where he stood.

His eyes bulging, he stared at the bear, sure any moment it would swing one of its mighty paws and that would be the end of it. He didn't want to die; he had so many dreams left unfulfilled.

Again, a voice in his mind screamed, Run! But he could not.

Images from his nightmare became real. In the nightmare, the dark priests had come for him and, like now, he had been unable to run. In the dream, blue flames conjured from his fright and desperation had lashed out at the priests. The priests had merely laughed and still they had taken him.

As if conjured again from his fear and desperation, the

forbidden magic came. Vilmos felt a prickling sensation—raw energy—in his fingertips. In his mind, he screamed No! at himself and the bear. What if this was the one time too many? What if this was the time that made the dark priests come for him? Then he asked himself the final what if. What if the bear charged now?

One swipe of its powerful paw was all it would take to end his young life. The girl from Olex Village had been taken nearly so.

What *had* the village huntsmen said about bears? Had the girl not run when she should have? Or ran when she shouldn't have? Vilmos couldn't remember. He stared directly at the bear. It was sniffing the air as if insulted that it was crosswinds from him. Then suddenly it dropped to all fours—Vilmos was sure this was it, this was the end. The bear would charge, swipe and he would die.

The bear roared.

Vilmos squeezed his eyes tight. A scream built in his throat, but died as it escaped his lips.

ABOUT THE AUTHOR

 Robert Stanek is the author of many previously published books, including several bestsellers. Currently, he lives in the Pacific Northwest with his wife and children. Robert is proud to have served in the Persian Gulf War as a combat crewmember on an electronic warfare aircraft. During the war, he flew numerous combat and combat support missions, logging over two hundred combat flight hours.

His distinguished accomplishments during the Persian Gulf War earned him nine medals, including the United States of America's highest flying honor, the Air Force Distinguished Flying Cross. His career total was 17 medals in only 11 years of military service, making him one of the most highly decorated veterans of the Persian Gulf War.

Overwhelmingly, readers agree that Robert's books are among the best they've ever read. His books have very vocal supporters who aren't afraid to voice their opinion, and they frequently do so in online communities and lists, such as at Amazon.com, where you'll find that his books are consistently listed at the top of their class. Strong reader support has led to strong sales. The worldwide in print total for his books is quickly approaching 2 million.

Visit www.robertstanek.com to learn more!

ABOUT REAGENT PRESS

Reagent Press is a small press that publishes both fiction and non-fiction titles. Current fiction titles include *Keeper Martin's Tale* and *Elf Queen's Quest* from the Ruin Mist Chronicles, *The Kingdoms & The Elves of the Reaches Book I* and *Book II* from Keeper Martin's Tales, and *The Elf Queen & The King Book I* and *Book II* from Ruin Mist Tales. Current non-fiction titles include: *Effective Writing for Business, College & Life*, *Essential Windows 2000 Commands Reference*, and *Essential Windows XP Commands Reference*.

Thank you for your continued support! Without the help of you, the reader, we will not be able to produce future works. If you liked this book, please tell your friends!

Visit www.tvpress.com online!

Ruin Mist Heroes, Legends & Beyond

Just about everyone that has read about Ruin Mist has wondered about the back story, where it all began, how the story all fits together, and now you can find answers in *Ruin Mist Heroes, Legends & Beyond*, a companion volume to the top-selling Ruin Mist books. *Ruin Mist Heroes, Legends & Beyond* allows you to learn about the dark elves of Under-Earth, common trades in the kingdoms, and beasts that go bump in the night. You can read the complete rules for King's Mate: the game, explore dozens of maps detailing the known realms, learn about the author, and more. In short, this is one book you shouldn't be without.

KEEPER MARTIN'S TALES

The Kingdoms & the Elves of the Reaches

Inside you'll discover the breathtaking world of Ruin Mist where the mystical and the magical abound, and you'll fall in love with a boy who would become a mage, a princess who is just now seeing the world around her, a warrior elf who undertakes an epic journey, and their friends.

The Kingdoms & the Elves of the Reaches 2

Adrina, Emel, Vilmos, Galan and Seth must survive the greatest challenge Great Kingdom has faced in hundreds of years: the dissolution of the Kingdom Alliance and the battle to save Quashan'. Survival in a changing world depends on their ability to adapt and if they fail, their world and everything they believe in will perish.

The Kingdoms & the Elves of the Reaches 3 & 4

Adrina, Emel, Vilmos, Galan and Seth face even greater challenges as their world is transformed. Vilmos, in his quest to become the first human magus in a thousand years, must control the darkness within him. Adrina  must accept her place and work together with Emel to help the elves make their plea to Great Kingdom's council. What happens along the way will amaze you.

IN THE SERVICE OF DRAGONS

The direct continuation of The Kingdoms &
the Elves of the Reaches!

RUIN MIST TALES

For every fantastic story you'll ever find there are often other stories that retell the adventures from different points of view—so why should it be any different in Ruin Mist? Join us now as we walk the dark path through the chronicles of Ruin Mist. Discover new secrets, new dangers, new visions and new realities!

MAGIC LANDS

Following the village elder's advice, Ray leaves his home village, setting out for the place lost and deep where he will find a companion for his journey to the stone land and where he will discover that there is no easy path from childhood to manhood. "Beware lashing tail and gnashing teeth," the village elder warns him, "and if Old Bull doesn't get you, Mother Slither surely will."

www.ingramcontent.com/pod-product-compliance
Lightning Source LLC
Chambersburg PA
CBHW071258130626
46556CB00003B/1370